The Cowboy's Final Ride

Cowboys of Whistle Rock Ranch, Book Four

Contemporary Western Romance

SHIRLEEN DAVIES

Books Series by Shirleen Davies

<u>Historical Western Romances</u>

Redemption Mountain

MacLarens of Fire Mountain Historical

MacLarens of Boundary Mountain

<u>Romantic Suspense</u>

Eternal Brethren Military Romantic Suspense

Peregrine Bay Romantic Suspense

<u>Contemporary Western Romance</u>

Cowboys of Whistle Rock Ranch

MacLarens of Fire Mountain Contemporary

Macklins of Whiskey Bend

The best way to stay in touch is to subscribe to my newsletter. Go to my Website *www.shirleendavies.com* and fill in your email and name in the
Join My Newsletter boxes. That's it!

Avalanche Ranch Press, LLC
PO Box 12618
Prescott, AZ 86304

Book design and conversions by Joseph Murray at 3rdplanetpublishing.com

Cover design by Sweet 'n Spicy Designs

ISBN: 978-1-947680-85-2

I care about quality, so if you find something in error, please contact me via email at shirleen@shirleendavies.com

Description

He's a rodeo cowboy seeking one more ride. She's the chef on a dude ranch. Can their two ingredient dish end in love?

Jake Kelman agreed to delay resuming his rodeo career to be a dude ranch cowboy. Herding cattle, fighting away wild dogs, and breaking horses are all in a day's work. His attraction to the ranch's cute and feisty chef isn't in his job description.

Beth Jenner left a coveted position at a high-class resort in Jackson to return home. How did she allow herself to land smack in the kitchen of a working dude ranch?

Recovering from a broken relationship, she's determined not to succumb to the too handsome cowboy who pops into her dreams each night.

When Beth learns Jake may leave sooner than expected, she forces herself to push aside her growing feelings to be the friend he needs.

Focusing his priorities on returning to the rodeo and buying a ranch of his own, Jake doesn't have time to nurture a relationship. Not even with the exact woman he's always wanted.

When danger appears, threatening not just his friends but the woman he cares so deeply for, Jake's priorities shift.

Will he set aside his dream of one final ride or capture a life bigger than he'd ever imagine?

The Cowboy's Final Ride, book four in the Cowboys of Whistle Rock Ranch Contemporary Western Romance series, is a clean and wholesome, full-length novel with an HEA.

The Cowboy's Final Ride

Chapter One

Whistle Rock Ranch
Late Fall

The crashing of snow slipping from the roof woke Jacob Kelman at the wicked hour of three in the morning. Another loud thump of breaking snow had him grabbing jeans from the floor. Spearing his legs into them, he slipped on yesterday's shirt before lifting a heavy coat and hat from hooks. Boots were almost an afterthought as he rushed to get outside.

Wind whipped in every direction, making visibility impossible. Squinting, Jake tried to make out lights from the main lodge or the bunkhouse. He couldn't see a single light.

The wind howled, accompanying a significant drop in temperature. Cold seeped through his thick coat, chilling him to the bone. Jake shifted with the intention of returning to his cabin when an ear-splitting scream stopped him. Human or a mountain lion, he wondered.

Sucking in a lungful of freezing air, he cupped his hands around his mouth. "Hello!"

A second scream answered him. This time, there was no doubt it was human.

Rushing inside, he grabbed a shotgun, filling his pockets with ammunition. Before heading back outside, he switched the original coat and boots with those meant for sub-zero weather.

This time, the glare of flashlights bounced along the snow covered ground as a group of men approached. Each one held a rifle or shotgun.

"Did you hear the screams, Virgil?"

The foreman of Whistle Rock Ranch nodded at Jake. "Thought it was a mountain lion. Now, I'm not so sure."

"The last one was human. I'm certain of it." All eyes landed on Wyatt Bonner, the manager and part owner of the ranch.

"How do you want us to move out?" Jeramy Barrel, a longtime ranch hand, blinked several times before wiping snow from his face.

Wyatt nodded at Virgil to take the lead. "Split into two teams. You've all been through this before, but I'll review the rules. Stay together. No more than three feet between each man. Confirm you have three flares apiece. I have extras. Barrel and I have satellite phones, so we'll lead the two teams. Jake, you're with me. Questions?" When none came, he waved a hand in the air. "Barrel's team will sweep toward the north, and we'll do the same going south."

Jake fell in beside Virgil at the same time another ear-piercing scream stopped them in their tracks. "I think it came from the rocks to our south."

Virgil nodded. "You may be right. Barrel! We'll need horses."

Once they'd tacked up their horses, the men spread out, all moving toward a hill to the southwest. The cluster of large boulders surrounded by tall pines was a favorite perch of various predators. Over the years, mountain lions, wolves, and bears had frequented the area for short periods of time.

Drawing closer, the group halted as another scream, followed by a shout for help, blasted from up ahead. Jake didn't have to look at the men to know they wanted to charge forward.

"Stay where you are," Virgil warned before cautiously moving toward the sound. He stopped when Wyatt joined him. The ranch hands watched as the two had an animated discussion. It ended when Virgil broke left toward the boulders and Wyatt broke right, motioning for the men to hold their positions.

Frustrated, Jake shifted toward Barrel. "Why are they leaving us behind?"

"Those two grew up together on this ranch. They know every inch of land, where animals hide, and all the trails. They won't hesitate to signal us when they have a better idea of what's happening."

Jake understood. Still, he didn't like staying behind.

Virgil and Wyatt disappeared behind thick-trunked trees and mammoth boulders for long minutes. Several rifle shots rang out, causing a few of the men to move forward.

Barrel shouted toward them. "You heard the order. If you want to continue working at Whistle Rock, you'd best heed it."

Frustrating minutes passed before Wyatt emerged, waving for men to join him. "We have a situation." He glanced over his shoulder. "Barrel, ride back and return with one of the ranch trucks. Throw blankets in the back, and include one of the large first aid kits. And call for an ambulance. Let them know three people need transport to the hospital. The rest of you stay here and keep your guns ready." Barrel kicked his horse into a gallop.

Jimmy French, one of the youngest ranch hands, leaned over his saddlehorn. "What are we looking for, boss?"

"I don't know for certain. We'll figure it out once we get some injured hikers back to the lodge. I'm going back to help Virgil. Jake, you're with me."

Jake kept his hand on the butt of his rifle while following Wyatt along a narrow trail into the woods. He assumed they wanted his help due to his paramedic training. Though he'd never worked in the field, Jake had graduated at the top of his class.

The knowledge helped several times during his rodeo days. He assumed it helped Wyatt and Virgil decide to hire him as a replacement for Trace Griffin, who now lived on his ranch in northern Wyoming with his wife and son.

Following Wyatt, he reined his horse around a large boulder, jaw dropping at the sight before him. Three people lay on the ground, blood soaking through bandages Virgil applied.

It was then Jake recalled someone telling him the foreman had a good deal of medical training. Dismounting, Jake grabbed a small first aid kit from his saddlebag, then dropped down to get a better look at the hikers.

"I'm ninety percent certain we're dealing with a pack of wild dogs."

Jake sent a disbelieving look at Virgil. "Wild dogs?"

"That's my guess from studying the bite marks and tracks."

Leaning down to focus on the various injuries of one victim, Jake gave a slow nod. "Were you able to speak with any of them?"

"One woke up for a few seconds before losing consciousness again. Nothing I can see appears to be life-threatening, but there could be internal injuries. You should have some antiseptic in your kit. I've used what Wyatt and I had."

Opening his kit, Jake pulled out a plastic bottle, showing it to Virgil.

"That'll work. Use a little on the worst wounds for each of the hikers." Virgil smiled. "You know what to do."

"I wasn't trained to treat animal bites."

"The main thing to remember is animals have some pretty nasty bacteria they can pass along. It's important to sterilize the wounds. We've done about all we can. It's a blessing they're sleeping through it."

"Barrel must be back with the blankets." Wyatt pointed to the red flare overhead. "I'll get the men to bring them to us."

Before he swung back atop his horse, sirens signaled the arrival of at least one ambulance. "I'll guide the paramedics back here."

Watching Wyatt ride off, Jake felt a strong hand on his arm. Shifting to look at the young man on the ground beside him, their gazes locked.

"Wild dogs," the man choked out, his eyes wild with fear. "They're everywhere." He coughed again, his grip on Jake's arm tightening. "Watch... out."

Sipping coffee at a table outside the kitchen, Jake couldn't stop thinking about the terror in the young man's eyes. It had been an hour since the last of the ambulances drove off, and he couldn't seem to forget the man's warning.

Somewhere on Whistle Rock Ranch land, a pack of wild dogs wandered, searching for more victims. Jake had seen the same as a young boy. A pack of seven wild dogs terrorized his family's ranch and the town not far away. Three children and two adults were killed before authorities captured or killed the animals.

"Hey, Jake. Can I get you anything besides coffee?" Beth Jenner, the new assistant cook, stood next to the table.

"Coffee's fine. Thanks."

"Must've been pretty bad out there."

"Yeah, it was." Standing, he tossed out the last of his coffee. Setting the cup down, he walked off without another word.

Sweeping the cup into her hand, Beth watched him disappear into the barn.

Other than an occasional hello, she'd never gotten up the nerve to talk to him before. Jake kept to himself, spoke to ranch guests and male employees. Seldom did he speak with the women who lived on the ranch.

Beth had watched him for almost thirty minutes before stepping outside. It had been a mistake. She knew it would be a long time before she tried again.

Chapter Two

Jake shook off the irritation caused by the ranch's chef interfering with his personal thoughts. Couldn't she tell he wanted to be left alone? Some women had no common sense. Beth Jenner appeared to be one of those women.

Her working at the ranch never made sense to him. From what Virgil said, she'd graduated from a prestigious cooking school. Several job offers had followed, with her rising quickly to head chef at a high-end restaurant in Jackson, Wyoming.

She'd gone from diamonds and sports cars to little gold crosses and pickup trucks. Experience told him women didn't pick the latter unless something had gone terribly wrong. Beth Jenner must've had a real setback to end up as an assistant cook at a dude ranch.

Jake found himself chuckling on the last. Whistle Rock Ranch was a dude, or guest ranch. It was also one of the most profitable cattle and horse ranches in the western United States.

The ranch hands were some of the hardest working men he'd ever been around. Nothing was too hard, and he'd yet to hear any of them griping about an order from Virgil or Wyatt. They simply got the job done, much like those working the rodeo circuit.

Tacking up his horse, Jake couldn't help thinking about the life he'd left behind. It was a life he loved and hoped to return to before growing too old to compete.

According to the doctor, he already was too old. Good thing he wasn't the kind of man who believed what the docs told him. His destiny was within his control, not in the hands of a medical professional who rushed to treat twenty patients each day.

"Jake, you're with Wyatt, Barrel, and me today."

"Are we going after the dogs?"

"We're going to look for tracks. Maybe we can figure out what direction they went."

"They could be anywhere by now, boss."

"Yeah, I know. Still, I have a lot of questions about what happened to those hikers."

Jake turned to face Virgil, unsettled by his words. "Questions?"

"I'm fairly certain at least one member of the pack is carrying rabies."

"Rabies? That would mean those hikers could be infected. Not good news." While in high school, a friend of Jake's was bitten by a rabid bat. The cure wasn't pleasant, but at least his friend lived.

"I doubt the hospital will tell me if any of them contracted rabies, but…"

Jake smiled at the expression on Virgil's face. "With your wife a nurse there, she might be able to find out."

Virgil choked out a strained laugh. "It's a touchy situation with the privacy regulations. All I want to do is protect those at the ranch and our neighbors. If one of the dogs is a carrier, we'll be forced to locate the pack."

Virgil didn't need to say more. If the pack was infected, there would be no option other than putting them down. It wasn't an action any of them wanted, but protecting the area from a rabid pack of wild dogs had to be their first priority.

Wyatt and Barrel joined them, their horses already tacked up and ready to ride. "Do you have a plan, Virg?" Wyatt swung into the saddle, reining his mount toward the area where they'd found the hikers.

"We'll be looking for tracks. I want to know where the pack went after attacking the hikers. What direction are they moving? About how many wild dogs are in the pack? I'm not planning to confront them until we know if one or more is infected with rabies."

Wyatt's jaw tightened. "Pop called Gabe Montez." He mentioned a doctor at the hospital who had worked on the ranch in high school. Montez owed much of his medical schooling to funds set aside by Anson Bonner. "Two of the hikers tested positive for rabies."

The men fell silent, digesting the new information. Each knew it meant a change in this afternoon's ride.

"I want everyone to carry a rifle, shotgun, and handgun, plus ammo for all three. We don't know the size of the pack, and everyone should be prepared." Virgil walked his horse out of the barn. "Go ahead and get what you need. I'll grab food from Beth."

"I'll get it, Virgil." Jake handed the foreman his reins before walking toward the kitchen, wondering what had motivated him to volunteer. "It's just food," he said out loud, garnering looks from two ranch hands who passed by him. If he wasn't careful, the men were going to think him tetched in the head.

Rapping twice on the kitchen door, he stepped inside to find Beth wrapping food in storage bags. She shot him a questioning look before placing the bags in a fabric pouch.

"I assume you're here for this." She held out the pouch.

"Yes, ma'am."

The corners of her mouth twitched upward. "Please, call me Beth."

He stared at her a moment before deciding she was playing with him. "Got it. You can call me Jake."

"Jake it is. I'd better get back to my work. Lots to do with Nacho visiting his brother in Arizona."

A brow raised. "I didn't know he'd left."

"Yesterday afternoon. His brother is recovering from surgery. Nacho doesn't expect to be gone long."

Nodding, the moment became awkward when neither had anything else to say. Clearing his throat, his hand landed on the knob of the back door.

"I'll let you get back to work. Thanks for the food."

"Anytime, Jake." She turned away before he could see her grin.

Heading straight for his horse, he scratched the back of his neck. There was something about Beth Jenner which intrigued and frustrated him. Intrigued because he had a sense she was an interesting woman with many layers. Frustrated because he didn't plan to be here more than a year. Just long enough to heal from his last injury before returning to the life of a rodeo cowboy.

Any doctor would tell him going back would invite another injury, which would most likely result in paralysis. Jake knew he'd already pushed his body to its limit. He'd reached the pinnacle of his career, earned numerous titles, and made enough money to live comfortably for the rest of his life. Then why this throbbing desire to go back for one more season?

Sliding the food into a saddlebag, he forced himself to think of something else. Such as the pack of wild dogs they were hunting. Or why his tongue tangled in a knot when he was near Beth. Ignoring the last, he decided focusing on the search was a much safer option.

"You ready, Jake?" Wyatt sat atop his horse, looking out into the distance. Virgil and Barrel were close by, their gazes locked on their destination.

Swinging into his saddle, he nodded. "Let's go."

Beth finished cleaning the kitchen before starting dinner, smiling at the routine. It had become seamless. Each meal rolled into the next, leaving little time to mourn the mistakes of the past.

This job had been a godsend. A disastrous relationship with the owner of the upscale resort and four-star restaurant where she worked in Jackson had ended after what had been three glorious years. At least they'd been glorious to Beth. The man she'd thought of as a partner had transferred his affections to a young masseuse. Under the circumstances, leaving had been the best choice.

The timing was perfect when Virgil approached her about the position. Although she grew up in Brilliance, they'd met while attending the University of Wyoming. She'd gone on to culinary school, growing her career with each new job.

Over those years, her mother's health had deteriorated to where she worked one part-time job
instead of the three she'd held while Beth and her brothers were growing up. A good woman with a generous heart, Beth couldn't allow her to continue the grueling work of cleaning offices. She deserved to retire.

With her brothers living out of state, Beth returned to Brilliance for the new job and to help their mother. It was her chance to start over, forgetting the mistakes of the past.

Opening the refrigerator, she removed a large pot of her special chicken stew for lunch. She'd suggested the recipe to Nacho, who'd encouraged her to make it while he was gone. Setting it on the commercial stove, she turned on the oven. She'd learned letting it set, then warming it slowly enhanced the flavors. Beth would prepare cornbread with cheddar cheese and jalapeños, and a salad to go with the stew.

Measuring out the ingredients for the cornbread, she folded everything together before slicing almost microscopic slices of jalapeño. Adding them, she set pans on the counter, filling each with the mixture. Normally, she'd bake them in individual iron skillets. The ranch didn't have enough, so large baking pans would have to do.

Checking the time, Beth set out utensils, plates, napkins, and pitchers of water. Cookies, brownies, and carrot cake were also placed on the buffet table, with plenty of time left before the men appeared.

The phone in her pocket rang, interrupting her routine. She didn't recognize the number, was about to ignore it, then changed her mind.

"Hello?"

"Hi, Beth."

Her body stiffened at the familiar voice. She never should've answered. Anger began to replace fear.

"How did you get this number?"

"You know I have resources. How are you?"

"I'm hanging up now. Don't call again." Beth touched the end button, her hand shaking. Before she could put the phone away, it rang again. This time, she ignored it.

"Time to get a new number."

"Are you talking to me?"

Beth jumped. Turning around, she placed a hand against her chest. "You scared me, Daisy."

"Sorry. I should've let you know I'd come inside."

"No reason for you to. I had my mind on something else or you wouldn't have startled me. Did you take the afternoon off?"

"Yep. I have a couple of people who are reliable and great with customers. The truth is, they don't need me there."

Daisy, an accomplished photographer and jewelry maker, owned a successful art store in downtown Brilliance. Her work, as well as those of other Wyoming artists, was displayed for sale.

"There's another reason I'm home early." Daisy placed a hand on her flat stomach, meeting Beth's expectant gaze.

"Oh my gosh. You're pregnant?"

A huge grin spread across Daisy's face. "You're the third person to know, and Wyatt isn't the first. I told Margie and Lily." She mentioned her mother-in-law and best friend, Virgil's wife. "I plan to tell Wyatt tonight."

"That's so exciting. How can I help?"

Daisy tapped a finger against her lips. "I'm thinking of an intimate dinner with music."

"Do you know where?"

"One of the empty guest cabins."

"We're having beef enchiladas for dinner, which Wyatt loves."

"Yes, he does, and it's perfect for my announcement."

"Great. Do you need help decorating the cabin?"

"I have that covered." Giving Beth a quick hug, Daisy rushed to the door. "Six o'clock okay?"

"Whatever works for you. I'll have everything in warming plates and placed in the cabin before then. And congratulations, Daisy. You two will make great parents."

Chapter Three

"What did you find?" Wyatt knelt down beside Virgil, who studied tracks in the snow covered dirt. Not responding, he moved to another set a couple feet away. Several other tracks caught his attention before he stood.

"These are pretty fresh, Wyatt. They're heading northwest. The bad news is there appear to be at least seven. Could be more."

"I haven't seen a pack of wild dogs since I was maybe eight."

"We were both eight, Wyatt. They carried rabies, the same as this pack." Virgil pointed to the tracks. "Our fathers made us stay inside until the pack was tracked down."

"Both of us cried when we learned they had to put the dogs down."

"It may be the same with this pack. At least one dog is infected. They've already transmitted the rabies to two hikers. The county health department is sending alerts out to all the other counties."

"The entire state?"

Virgil nodded. "My guess is the pack's region is western Wyoming. I believe it's better to be safe and cast a wide net."

"You're right."

"What did you guys find?" Barrel bent down to see what had caught their attention.

Beside him, Jake studied the numerous tracks. "Definitely a sizable group of wild dogs."

Virgil brushed his hands together before standing and wiping them down his jeans. Pointing to the tracks, he walked several yards away.

"The pack is moving northwest. Or they were when these tracks were made."

Jake knelt down to study the imprints more closely. "How old?"

"Hours." Virgil walked a few more feet before turning back. "What do you want to do, Wyatt?"

"Follow them for another hour. Maybe we'll get lucky and find their home."

From what Wyatt had learned, a pack of wild dogs was rare in the U.S. More common were packs of gray wolves who descended from domestic dogs. He looked at Virgil.

"Could they be gray wolves?"

"Makes sense. Wild dog packs aren't common, but there are some."

Jake's brows drew together "What do you mean, Virgil?"

"Those packs are made up of dogs that have been abandoned. Over time, they formed a pack with other displaced dogs. They establish their own den, and hunt the same as gray wolves, which are also considered wild dogs. The hikers may have gotten a good look at them and can clarify for us."

Wyatt rubbed the back of his neck. "Gray wolves are now federally protected."

"But if they're carrying rabies?" Barrel asked.

Virgil began walking toward the horses. "I'll talk to someone at the game and fish department. My understanding is they aren't protected in Wyoming. Even if they are, a rabid pack is a danger to everyone. Game and fish will have to deal with them."

Beth removed the last pies from the oven, placing them on a cooling rack. The two roasts had another hour in the oven before she shredded them for enchiladas. A man who favored his own recipes, even Nacho loved the variation she'd prepared within a week of arriving. The secret was in the spices, which she graciously shared with the longtime head cook.

"Smells wonderful in here. Is it the meat for tonight's enchiladas?" Daisy glanced around, not seeing what would cause the dazzling aroma. "It's not the pies."

Chuckling, Beth nodded toward the oven. "I'm cooking two roasts."

"He loves your enchiladas." Placing a hand on her stomach, Daisy shot a knowing look at Beth. "I hope he'll be happy about it."

"Are you kidding? The man will be over the moon." Something Beth didn't want to define washed over her. She let the mood pass before smiling at Daisy. "You're still telling him tonight, right?"

"I am. Having a baby isn't something I can keep to myself for long. Lily helped me decorate the cabin before leaving for her shift at the hospital. It looks beautiful. I'm going to take a shower and dress. Maybe the hot water will help me relax."

"Let me know if there's anything else you need. I'm happy to help."

"Thanks, Beth. Wish me luck!"

You won't need it, Beth thought as Daisy left. Shaking off the melancholy which overtook her less and less each day, she checked the roasts.

"Almost perfect."

Busying herself preparing the rest of the meal, her mind drifted back to her days at the University of Wyoming. She hadn't planned to attend culinary school when entering college. Her love had been studying U.S. history. Then she'd been offered a job in the kitchen of an Italian restaurant near campus.

The cooking bug had bitten her within a few days. Family owned, the wife had come from northern Italy, while her husband had been raised in the south. Combining food from both regions, their restaurant had experienced success from the day they'd opened. Best of all, they were more than willing to share their knowledge with Beth.

She'd been a sponge, soaking up the way they used herbs and spices, the types of pasta which worked best with specific sauces, how to prepare fish, and anything else the couple shared. When she'd graduated, quitting her job to attend culinary school, they'd handed her a notebook filled with family recipes. Beth hadn't been able to hold back the tears.

In the time since, she'd gathered her own recipes into a separate file on her computer. Tonight's beef enchiladas was one of those.

"Something smells terrific."

Her body went on alert at the now familiar voice. Glancing up from where she sliced tomatoes for pico de gallo, her mouth tipped up into a grin.

"Hello, Jake. Just get back?"

He nodded, snagging a corn chip from a bowl on the prep counter.

"Hey. That's for dinner."

Grabbing a few more, he shrugged. "Might be best to put them out a few minutes before everyone arrives." Whirling around, he started for the door.

"You're leaving already?" She tried to keep any trace of disappointment from her voice. Disappointment which stunned her.

"Yep." He waved a hand before closing the door behind him.

"Strange man." Beth shook her head as she diced an onion. Yet there was something about him which she found intriguing. Her hands stilled on the thought.

She'd been devastated when her relationship in Jackson fell apart. Beth had no desire to step into another one. Especially not with a way too handsome cowboy.

Work and time alone were where she now found peace. Walking the numerous trails, which blanketed Whistle Rock Ranch, had become her respite, a way to clear her mind while considering her future.

She'd taken the assistant cook job until figuring out her next move. With her mother's fragile condition, Beth knew she'd have to stay close to Brilliance, which limited her choices.

Thankfully, Beth had been surprised how much she enjoyed working in the ranch kitchen. It had been the right decision to accept the position with a few weeks left in the guest ranch calendar. The long hours and interaction with vacationers of all ages helped her forget the pain of leaving Jackson.

Nacho allowed her to test many of her recipes on the guests. All had been accepted with great enthusiasm. Freddie had never let her place any of what he called her *concoctions* on the menu in Jackson, believing they were too pedestrian for such an upscale restaurant. As the owner, his word had been final.

Conjuring up an image of the man she used to date, Beth was shocked when she felt nothing. No anger. No regret. No pain. When had she turned the corner, leaving Freddie and his hurtful actions behind?

She didn't know, and cared even less. It was as if a heavy weight had been lifted from her, freeing her to breathe for the first time in months.

Jake brushed the red-gold tail and mane of his quarter horse gelding. The animal had been his partner since high school graduation, traveling with Jake from one rodeo to another. All his titles and every penny he'd earned came atop Cisco. With any luck, there'd be at least one more win before they retired for the final time.

"Beth is making her beef enchiladas for dinner." Barrel leaned against a post, watching as Jake finished cleaning Cisco's hooves. "You had her enchiladas?"

"At least twice."

"They're epic. I'm going to be the first in line."

Chuckling, Jake straightened. "Do you ever think of anything other than food?"

"Not on enchilada night. She makes this incredible salsa with just enough jalapeño for a slow burn." Barrel's stomach growled loud enough for Jake to hear.

"Maybe you should see if Beth will let you eat early."

"Are you kidding? She's a great cook but guards her food with a warrior's intensity."

A deep laugh burst from Jake's throat. "Warrior?"

"You know what I mean. She's a fighter when it comes to protecting our meals."

Jake thought of the chip he'd pilfered from the bowl not an hour earlier. He guessed he should be thankful Beth hadn't chopped off his hand.

He was about to ask Barrel another question when the kitchen's back door crashed open. Beth stormed out, holding the phone to her ear, the expression on her face had him taking a few steps closer.

Though he couldn't hear what she was saying, the anger was obvious. His mother would say the woman was spitting mad. Jake took a few more steps closer to her, then stopped. Beth had ended the call. Taking a deep breath, she walked several paces away from the kitchen before staring down at the ground.

He wanted to go to her, ask if she was all right. Then he saw something that kept him rooted in place.

Beth swiped away what he guessed to be tears from both cheeks.

The woman who greeted everyone with a smile, fought her own demons. Similar to him, he doubted Beth shared her troubles. She was the type of person who tried to find a way to cope on her own. Again, much the same as him.

Standing firm, he continued to watch from his spot just inside the barn. Beth stared up at the darkened sky as if counting stars. After a few moments, her shoulders slumped. Turning, she seemed to draw herself up, as if fortifying for a battle. Maybe that was exactly what she was doing.

Watching as she disappeared inside, he struggled with what he could or should do. Before he could make a decision, Barrel slapped him on the shoulder.

"Dinner bell just rang. Let's get up there."

Forcing himself to move, he kept pace as they closed the distance to the lodge.

25

Chapter Four

Jake winced as the frigid cold of the ice pack seeped into the tender skin of his right knee. The same knee he'd injured during his last rodeo. An injury the doctor had pronounced as career ending. The pronouncement he'd never accepted.

"Heard you twisted your knee." Virgil pulled up a chair, his gaze assessing the mottled purple swelling. "Looks painful."

"Yeah," Jake grunted, adjusting the ice pack.

"How'd it happen?"

"Rookie mistake. My boot caught in the stirrup while moving a small group of cattle."

One of Virgil's brows lifted.

"All right. A young one took off. If we lost him in the snow, I knew we might not find him again. When I reined Cisco around, he slipped on an ice patch at the same time my boot caught in the stirrup. He danced around to gain traction. I lost my balance and…"

"Fell out of the saddle."

Jake shook his head. "Hasn't happened in years. Not since high school. Jimmy and Barrel helped me back on Cisco. I'm sure I'll be hearing about this for months."

Virgil couldn't hold back a grin. "Years. Those boys have long memories. Do you want me to have someone drive you to the hospital? Might be good to have it checked it."

"Nah. I've been through this before. The doctor will prescribe ice and pain meds, and a wrap. Won't stop me from working."

Rising, Virgil looked down at him. "You're off today and tomorrow, then we'll assess the knee again."

"That's right. You're kind of a medical whiz with ranch injuries."

"I'm better with animals," he snorted, opening the door. "I'll send Beth with food. There's a crutch somewhere. Don't try to walk without it for a couple days."

Giving a mock salute, Jake adjusted the ice pack once again as the door closed behind the ranch foreman. He'd lost concentration for a fraction of a second. A tiny fragment of time. The mistake resulted in him dealing with an injury to an already damaged knee.

Swinging his good leg onto the bed before lifting the injured one, he replaced the pack and reclined against the pillow. Jake knew he couldn't sleep, yet he closed his eyes anyway.

A loud rap on the door woke him from a fitful dream about spilling out of the saddle. Blinking, he pushed up, groaning at the pain in his knee. The knocking came again.

"Enter." Thinking it was Virgil with the crutch he'd promised, he adjusted his legs so he could sit on the edge of the bed. Instead, Beth stepped into the cabin carrying a tray laden with food.

Even though he wore long johns, he grabbed a blanket, draping it over his legs.

"Hope I'm not interrupting anything." She kicked the door closed with a booted foot before turning to face him. "How are you doing?"

"Been better. I'll be back at it tomorrow."

"That's not what Virgil says. You'll be lucky to get back on your horse for several days." Setting the tray on the small dining table, she began unwrapping the food. When finished, she dragged the table next to the bed.

"How come you rate a cabin and aren't in the bunkhouse with the other men?"

"Simple. I took over for Trace. This was his cabin."

She slid a large piece of cornbread, steaming bowl of stew, bottle of water, and utensils toward him. "Go ahead and eat while it's hot."

While he dug into the stew, she unwrapped the last item. A large slice of lemon cream pie. She'd noticed he hadn't let a single slice of the sweet/tart pie go to waste after previous dinners.

He swallowed a large forkful of stew while watching her. "Is that lemon pie?"

"It is. There was this one slice leftover. Hope you're interested."

"Heck, yes. I love your lemon pie."

"It's actually lemon cream. A little different from lemon meringue or lemon angel pie."

"I'm all-in for the slice you have right there."

She hid a grin at his enthusiasm. "You might change your mind after eating the stew and cornbread. That's quite a bit of food."

Finishing the last bite of cornbread, he shot her an unbelieving look. "I could've eaten twice this much and still be able to eat an entire pie."

"Big talk, cowboy."

"Hey. It's not just talk if it's true." He handed her the empty bowl, accepting the pie in exchange. "Hmmm. This is great. Is it your own recipe?"

"No. My mama didn't cook much."

"Really. Seems most people who are good cooks come from a family of good cooks."

"Not me. Boxed mac and cheese, fish sticks, noodles with butter and nothing else, and canned spaghetti were her specialties." Beth placed the dirty plates on the tray before crossing her arms. "I got my love of cooking after being hired by a restaurant near U of W. They were a great family and taught me all I know. Well, not all, but real close. Culinary school added more technical knowledge. In truth, if I didn't think cooking school would've been an asset on my resume, I would've opened my own restaurant after graduating from U of W. Well, there was the slight issue of having no money to open my own restaurant.”

“I see where that would be a problem.” Finishing the last of the pie, he handed the plate back to her. “Everything was great. Thanks.”

Tucking the plate next to the bowl, she picked up the tray. “Any requests for breakfast?”

“Whatever is on the menu is fine with me.”

“Pancakes with fruit compote, bacon, eggs, country potatoes, and biscuits.”

“All of it is good for me.”

A soft laugh left her lips as a smile brightened her eyes. The effect on Jake was immediate. He hadn’t experienced such an intense reaction to a woman in, well...he couldn’t recall how long it had been since he’d been attracted to any woman. Well before he’d messed up his knee as a rodeo competitor.

“Sounds good. I’ll be here as soon as possible. No later than seven-thirty.”

He didn’t meet her gaze, still reeling from the effect she had on him. “Whatever is good for you.”

Cocking her head, she studied him for a moment. “Okay. I’ll see you in the morning.” Stepping outside, she turned back toward him. “There’s a crutch out here. I assume it’s for you.”

“Virgil said he’d bring it over.” He wondered why the foreman hadn’t brought it inside, but let it go. Putting distance between him and Beth had become his main priority.

Balancing the tray with one hand, she brought the crutch inside, placing it next to the bed. "Here you are. Do you want to give it a try before I leave?"

"No." He winced at the startled look on Beth's face. "I mean, I've used one before, so it's not going to be a problem."

"Then I'll get out of your hair." Without glancing back, she left, softly closing the door behind her.

"Geez." Jake hung his head, feeling bad about how he'd snapped at her. Yet the response was an honest response to how she affected him.

"You're overreacting to a woman's smile," he muttered at the same time he reached for the crutch. "Nothing more."

His fingers brushed the aluminum frame, tipping the crutch enough so it fell to the floor with a metallic thud. Biting back his frustration, Jake scooted forward, bending at the waist to retrieve it.

Placing the crutch close by, he rubbed his tired eyes. He had plans, and they didn't include being sidetracked by a bright, attractive woman. His future wasn't working on Whistle Rock Ranch.

Trace had offered Jake a job at his ranch whenever his friend needed one. The only person to know his dream of one more year rodeoing, Jake knew the offer was sincere. The odds were he'd take his friend up on the offer. But that was a good year or two in the future.

When he did leave, Jake would leave Wyatt and Virgil with a recommendation for a well-qualified replacement. He already had someone in mind. A mutual friend of his and Trace had already decided to leave his job as foreman of a small ranch in Idaho. A place the size of Whistle Rock would fit his needs, and Jake had no doubt he'd jump at the chance to make a change.

All of this meant Jake falling for any woman was out of the question. A complete and absolute impossibility.

"Are you going to be able to stay in the saddle, Sugarfoot?"

Jake sent Barrel a nasty look before landing atop Cisco. It had been a week since his accident. If Virgil hadn't given his approval to get back to work, Jake would've gotten on his horse and ridden anyway. Where didn't matter. One more day inside the cabin and he would've gone nuts from staring at four walls, and from trying to ignore Beth more when she brought his meals.

Unlike the first day, she hadn't shared anything about herself. She'd unwrap his food, leave, and return thirty minutes later to pick up the dirty dishes. Exchanging greetings and pleasantries, neither tried to lead them into a deeper conversation. Jake wondered if she fought the same attraction which plagued him.

Barrel, Jimmy, Jake, and two other ranch hands were heading north to bring in a small herd of cattle. Jake slid in beside Barrel, taking one more glance over his shoulder toward the lodge. Beth stood in the kitchen doorway, one shoulder rested against the doorjamb. Her gaze locked with his for an instant before she whirled around, closing the door behind her.

"Nice lady. Great cook and good-looking. You could do a lot worse."

"What are you talking about now, Barrel?"

"The cook. And don't go saying I'm nuts."

"Well, everyone knows you're nuttier than a brownie loaded with walnuts." Jake searched for an answer which would silence the conversation. "She's been bringing meals. Neither of us talk much. That's all there is to it."

"So you say."

Jake sat straighter in the saddle, adjusting his right foot in the stirrup. "Yeah, I do say. Where are we going?"

"North."

"Virgil told me that much. Where exactly?"

"We've got a small herd north of the lodge. The boss wants them closer."

Jake gave a slow nod. "If we come across the wild dogs, I won't hesitate to protect the herd...and us."

"No one expects anything different."

They rode in silence for close to thirty minutes before Barrel spoke again. "I hope you stick it out. Not that I blame Trace for wanting his family back. Emma is terrific, and Koa, well...that boy is a whirlwind of energy. Real smart too. Anyway, Trace was great with the guests. So far, you've shown you'll be as good as him. Maybe better."

"Why are you saying all this?"

"Because the ranch needs stability. You'll be second to Virgil, and in charge of making sure the guest activities are top-notch and run without a hitch. I'm just hoping you realize what a great opportunity the job is for you."

Jake let the man's words roll around in his head for a bit. "What about you?"

"What about me?"

"Why don't you take the job?"

Barrel threw his head back on an explosive laugh. "Because I'm tongue-tied when around the guests. I can lead a trail ride. But if a guest has a problem? That's not me. I'd rather talk to the horses than the guests. Trust me. There aren't many who can do what you can and have the patience to deal with the guests' problems. Just letting you know how much this ranch needs and counts on you, Jake."

Chapter Five

Julian Jenner drummed his fingers on his highly polished mahogany desk. He'd finished all the important matters hours earlier, leaving him with too much time to ponder his current situation.

As the president of Emerald Whole Foods, he should be visiting restaurants, talking to cooks, and gathering information about competitors. Instead, he spent hours pondering his next move rather than acting on the data right in front of him.

There were three smaller companies similar to his in different parts of the country ripe for the picking. They didn't have the money to expand. Buying one or more of them would open up markets it would take years to build from scratch.

Julian knew he should trigger the acquisition of the company based in the northwest. One problem existed. The owner had learned of his interest and hired a firm to do a background check on him. A deep search which brought to light an issue Julian couldn't afford to have exposed.

Emerald's vice president of operations, a man trusted by not only Julian, but his board of advisors, had been keeping costs low by inking deals with farms whose products weren't technically organic.

An employee had discovered the man's deceit when she visited two of the farms while on vacation. Casual conversations with the owners had unearthed the fact they sometimes used pest control measures not strictly organic. She hadn't brought up the fact their agreements with Emerald had them certify to certain standards. Agreements the farmers were breaking by using control methods which weren't organic.

The day she returned from vacation, the woman bypassed her boss and went straight to Julian. An investigation of other growers discovered one more who sometimes used unacceptable methods. All insisted the head of operations knew about what they believed to be a non-issue.

Reminded of the non-disclosure agreements they'd signed, the vice president of operations and his assistant had been let go. All three growers vowed to change their methods, and passed recertification.

A year later, all seemed fine except for the unsettling phone calls at all hours of the day and night. Julian and his wife believed they knew who made the stalkerish calls. They'd been diligent in taping them for police review.

The caller had been prepared. Using throwaway phones and digitally altering his voice, there'd been nothing the police could do. Plus, as Julian was reminded whenever he contacted his friend in the department, the caller had never made a direct threat. The calls were unsettling but posed no immediate danger to Julian's family.

From the beginning of the investigation, he'd kept the incident restricted to a handful of people. Julian saw no reason to worry others about what he'd come to regard as an inconvenience rather than a threat.

Picking up one of the offers to acquire a company in Washington state, the phone rang. Julian stared at it, knowing who would be at the other end of the call.

"There they are." Jake pointed toward a scattered herd of cattle eating the last of the hay delivered by a couple ranch hands. "Bringing them closer is a real good idea."

"I agree." Jimmy leaned over the saddlehorn. "It'll make feeding them easier."

Barrel nodded his agreement. "And it'll be easier to protect them from predators such as the wild dog pack."

Jake's brows scrunched together. "Why weren't they driven in earlier?"

"Snow came earlier this year. We'd normally wait another week or two, but with the storms predicted, we have to get it done now."

Rounding them up, Jake had an easy time getting into his own thoughts, as the return trip took much longer. His knee had bothered him since mounting Cisco outside the barn. The pain didn't matter. Getting back to work cleared his head, allowing him to think more clearly.

Barrel's comments bothered him. There'd never been a doubt the ranch hand's loyalty was to the brand. Had been since the day he'd been hired.

Jake understood. Under normal circumstances, his loyalty would be to Whistle Rock Ranch. If he wasn't so caught up in his need to ride one more time, he'd feel the same as Barrel. Not that he wouldn't give it a hundred percent, because he would. Quitting didn't set well with him. He had to find a solution that could work for everyone.

An image of Beth popped into his head. He liked her a lot. If circumstances were different, he'd be spending more time with her, may have already asked her out. Other than her beauty and incredible personality, she had a sweet soul, a person who once committed would show total devotion.

Thinking of Beth had his mind wandering to another woman he knew. Someone he'd loved unconditionally. Jake thought she felt the same, yet she'd chosen someone else. When that relationship fell apart, she'd turned to Jake for comfort and alcohol to erase the pain.

To his credit, he hadn't turned away. Maybe he'd hoped to rekindle what he thought they'd once shared. Perhaps he was just being a friend. Jake didn't know what had motivated him to stick by her for so long. After months of showing little desire to stop drinking, he'd had to let her go. Her parents had taken over, which may have been the best solution from the start.

The idea of another relationship held little appeal. Not even with someone as wonderful as Beth.

They slowed to herd the cattle into a fenced pasture not far from the lodge. His phone rang about the time they were fifty yards from the barn. Without checking caller ID, he answered. The voice on the other end had him reining away from the others.

"Hello, Jake."

"Helena." His voice was flat, offering no welcome.

"Oh, Jake, don't be mad. Aren't you glad to hear from me?"

Letting out a strangled breath, his jaw clenched. "I'm busy, Helena. Why did you call?"

"I don't know exactly. It's been a while, and I miss you. Where are you?"

"I'm not getting into this with you, Helena."

She was quiet for over a minute before speaking again. "You were right. Drinking didn't help me deal with my problems. But I hardly drink at all anymore, Jake."

"How much is hardly? A drink a day? Two drinks?"

"No more than two drinks. Well, sometimes more, but it's much less than when you were here. So you see, I'm doing better."

"You need to stop completely, Helena."

"That's what my parents and counselor say. It's just so hard."

"You're a strong woman. You can stop if you want to bad enough. It's all up to you."

"I could do it if you were here, Jake," she whispered.

And there it was, the real reason for her call. "You know I can't be there. This is something you have to do on your own."

"I still love you, Jake."

It was a punch to his gut, her way of getting to him. He ignored the pain it caused. "I have to get back to work, Helena."

"And I guess I'll have another drink." She hung up before Jake could say more.

Staring at the phone a long time, he wondered if there'd ever be a time when her voice didn't twist his heart. Trace told him getting away would help, as would time. Jake guessed enough time hadn't passed because nothing much had changed.

As far as her drinking, stopping was up to her. He'd done all he could, and nothing had helped. Until she wanted to quit, nothing would change.

Hearing his name being called, he reined Cisco around to see Barrel standing next to Virgil. Riding over, he slid to the ground, liftin his chin toward Virgil.

"Barrel said you didn't spot the wild dogs. Did you notice any tracks?"

"None. Doesn't mean they didn't pass through there." Jake felt the phone vibrate in his pocket. He ignored it. "But I don't believe so. They would've attacked the cattle if they were anywhere near them."

Virgil nodded. "I agree." Scratching the back of his neck, his lips twisted into a grimace. "I was hoping we'd get a sense of where they were headed."

Jake glanced between Virgil and Barrel. "This is a guess, but I think they went south."

"Why south?" Virgil asked.

"Less people, more wildlife, some cattle, lots of places for the pack to hide."

"You sound as if you know the area, Jake."

"I do, Virgil. An uncle used to take me hunting south of here when I was a kid. We went every year until the year I left for U of W. He passed during my freshman year."

"South would be better for us," Barrel said.

"They still have to be stopped. We can't have a rabid pack roaming southern Wyoming."

Jake shoved his hands into his pockets. "You're right, Virgil. What do you want us to do?"

"We want to find the pack before winter makes tracking too difficult." The local warden of the Wyoming Game and Fish department, Austin Crane, stood before a group of ranch hands and volunteer trackers. They'd gathered before sunrise on Whistle Rock Ranch.

"Groups will be made up of four men and women." Austin glanced at a group of women standing to the side, and nodded. "We'll be driving. We don't want to put any of your horses at risk. Plus, you can take more gear on a four-wheeler."

Austin took another fifteen minutes explaining the strategy prepared by the state department. After answering questions, the volunteers divided into eight groups. Four men from Whistle Rock Ranch made up one group, all new and eager to prove themselves to Wyatt and Virgil.

"This will be a one shot deal lasting no more than seventy-two hours. You'll all come back to the four base camps each afternoon. No exceptions. If your group doesn't show up by six, and can't be reached by radio, we'll assume you're in trouble and send out search and rescue. That's a big expense and will hold up the search, so be sure to get to base before six. Are there any other questions?"

When no one spoke up, Austin pointed to the sun rising in the east. "You're free to head out. Report in on schedule or we'll come looking for you."

Wyatt, Virgil, and Jake stood off to the side. They would be connected by radio to the group from Whistle Rock Ranch. All four ranch hands had tracking experience, two from their time in the Army.

"I sure hope this works." Wyatt watched his men climb into the Jeep Rubicon owned by the ranch.

Crossing his arms, Virgil's jaw clenched as their men waved at them before driving away. "They better come back in one piece. One of those men is a third cousin. His folks will kill me if he gets hurt."

"Yeah? Which one?" Jake asked.

"The one with the pony tail like mine." Virgil tried to curb the slight sarcasm. "He drove in late last night. His name's Brady Blackwolf. He's younger, with some experience, and eager to learn. Very quiet."

"More so than you?" Wyatt asked.

Virgil grinned. "A lot."

"I don't care how quiet he is as long as he can do the work. This will be a good test for him," Wyatt said. "And for the other three."

Jake watched their brake lights disappear into the early morning light, wishing he could go with them. As Virgil pointed out, he was needed at the ranch. It brought back Barrel's comments and how much the owners and ranch hands depended on him to stick around.

Jake didn't know if he could make a decision which would work for everyone.

Chapter Six

"You have to eat something, Mama." Beth held a steaming bowl of chicken with vegetable soup. "It's your favorite."

"I know it is, sweetheart, but I'm just not hungry." Donna Jenner rested her back against the headboard of her bed, a frown creasing the drawn lines of her forehead and eyes.

"You always say that, Mama. Then I find out you made yourself a big bowl of cold cereal. You cannot live on shredded wheat or corn flakes."

The older woman huffed out a heated breath. "I like them, and they don't bother my stomach."

"My soup doesn't bother your stomach, and it's much healthier."

Donna looked over her daughter's shoulder to see the home improvement show on the flat screen television. One of many gifts from Beth and her sons.

"Mama, this is important."

"So is what they're doing on my show. You could learn something if you watched the professionals on these fix your house shows."

Beth glanced around the master bedroom of the house where she and her brothers grew up. It had been painted and new plank flooring installed since she'd moved back to Brilliance. She and her brothers had also renovated her bath. Well, the guys had sent money and let Beth make all the decisions.

"I live in a cabin at the ranch."

"So?"

"It's owned by the Bonners. There's nothing I need to do to it."

"Then use the ideas in my house. Afterall, someday it will belong to you and the boys."

A wicked smile appeared on Beth's face. "All right. I'll stay a while and watch your show if you eat the soup."

"That's blackmail."

"Yep."

"Humph. Well, seems I don't have a choice if you're to stay for a bit. Hand it over."

Beth gave her the bowl while giving a slow shake of her head. Donna knew her daughter would've stayed as long as possible. The give and take had become a game. For Beth, the haggling was fun much of the time.

Today, tired from all the extra work she took on when Nacho left to visit his brother, all she wanted was to curl up in her bed and sleep a few hours. She'd give her mother an hour before driving back to the ranch.

Rushing to swallow a mouthful of soup, Donna pointed to the television. "Look at that. Have you ever seen anything as spectacular?"

Beth watched the show's hosts tour a home renovation in Texas. They'd done an outstanding job. Yet she'd been to quite a few amazing homes during her work as an executive chef.

"Stunning, Mama." Lowering herself into a nearby chair, Beth stretched out her legs, reaching for the ceiling with her arms. It felt good to relax, even if for only a little bit.

"Now, tell me if you are dating anyone."

"Dating? I don't even recall what that is. I'm working from sunrise to sunset. Wyatt and Virgil are grilling burgers and sausages. Guess they, and a couple ranch hands, do it every year." Jake and Barrel had volunteered to help, but her mother didn't need to know their names. She'd never remember them.

"Those men are insane. Don't they know it's snowing?"

"Of course they do, Mama. They erected a pop-up over the grill and tables."

"So, all they're having are burgers and sausages? Not much of a party."

Beth bit her lower lip to stifle a saucy retort. "One of the men made his famous ranch beans. His words, not mine. Another prepared potato salad, and I baked cookies and brownies."

"Well, I still think they're crazy for grilling during a snowstorm." Setting her empty bowl aside, she once again concentrated on her show. "Isn't that the nicest kitchen you've ever seen?"

"Gorgeous, Mama."

"How many men work at the ranch?"

The change in subject surprised Beth. "Twenty full-time and some part-timers. There are seasonal workers between April and September. The Bonners told me they added employees when they decided to run the guest ranch. It is quite the operation."

"And you still like working there?"

"Love it."

"I never thought you'd be satisfied there after leaving the high-end restaurant and resort in Jackson. Do you ever get bored making the same meals over and over?"

"I don't fix the same five or six meals. Nacho has allowed me to try new recipes a few times each week. So far, everyone loves what's been added."

Her mother sat up straighter on the bed. "Do they let you ride?"

Beth remembered her mother used to ride while growing up. She even had her own horse for several years. All that changed when she married Beth's father.

He was a wonderful husband and father until a drunk driver plowed into his truck, causing it to roll down an embankment and ram into a tree. Once they cut him from the wreckage and ran tests, the relatively young father of three learned he was paralyzed from his chest down.

If the trucking company he worked for hadn't provided full medical and disability coverage for employees with catastrophic injuries, they'd have lost everything.

Given all her father required and the expenses of a family with three children, Donna had worked two, sometimes three, jobs. When she and her brothers turned sixteen, each found work in town. Their supplemental earnings helped a great deal.

Everything had fallen into place until several years earlier when their father had died in his sleep. Beth had cried until there were no more tears left. All those years as a paraplegic hadn't changed his quick laugh or sharp mind. His death had been devastating.

"I'm sure they'd let me if I asked. Maybe I'll ride in the spring." She flashed Donna a brilliant smile. "You could ride with me."

Donna didn't respond, seeming to consider the idea. "Do you think I could?"

"I'm certain of it. That is, as long as your doctor gives her okay."

"She's a rider, darling. No way she'll keep me off a horse."

Beth wasn't so sure, but no use making an issue of it now. "You're probably right. I'll get one of the men to guide us around the trails."

Jake would be perfect, she thought, then shoved away the idea. Beth didn't need her mother figuring out she found the cowboy attractive. He wasn't right for her, and she definitely wouldn't fit what he wanted in a woman.

"Sounds wonderful, Beth. It will give me something to look forward to."

Her mother's comment sat heavy on Beth during the drive to the ranch. Donna had been a rock from the moment they learned of her father's injuries until he died. Then she'd deflated, the smile she'd kept in place fading a little more each day.

Friends had stuck around for a while before vanishing into their own lives, leaving Donna behind. Beth couldn't think of a single woman Donna could call a good friend. They'd all shifted into the acquaintance category.

She never met girlfriends for a night out, didn't attend church or participate in community events. Up by six each morning, Donna would work a shift at the diner at the south end of town, return home, and watch her shows.

Beth had to find ways to get her mother out and about. She'd start at Thanksgiving by inviting her to the Bonner open house. Since there were two beds in her cabin, Donna would be able to stay the night. Settling the first step in her head, she frowned at the sound of her phone.

Looking at the holder on her dash, ice raced through her veins. She knew in her gut the caller was a man she had no intention of talking to. Even using the electronic voice scrambler, she could tell it was a man. Ignoring it, she turned on the radio, losing herself in a country song.

The phone chimed again. A quick glance indicated the same caller as before. When it rang a third time, Beth lowered the volume before sliding it into her purse. She didn't know who the man was or why he chose to stalk her via the phone. Not for the first time, Beth wondered if she should report the calls to the sheriff. Perhaps she'd mention it to Virgil, or maybe Jake.

Suspecting it would be a waste of time, she vowed to think about it a little more before talking to anyone.

With Thanksgiving two weeks away, Beth decided to prioritize the planning of what had become a major event at Whistle Rock Ranch. Margie Bonner sat down with her after Nacho left to pass along information on Thanksgiving and Christmas.

They weren't just for family. Both were treated as open houses, where everyone who walked through the lodge entry was welcome. Meals such as these, with no more than a guess as to the number of guests, had to be planned with ultimate care.

Turkey, ham, and venison were what Margie suggested. Leftovers would be placed in the large freezer, with some going to the local community cupboard. Pies, cookies, brownies, and other desserts could be made days ahead and frozen. Pumpkin pie would be a requirement. Thankfully, she had a killer recipe. The best and easiest pie she'd ever made. Appetizers, vegetables, rolls, and salads were her next task.

Taking the last curve to the ranch, she blinked as bright, oncoming lights blinded her. Tapping her brakes, her hands tightened on the steering wheel as her SUV began to slide to the right. Careful not to overcorrect, she was able to slow down without sliding off the road.

When the bright lights flew past, relief washed over her. Somehow, she'd stayed in her lane, and the turn to the ranch was no more than fifty yards away. Almost home.

The last warmed her. She was almost home.

Chapter Seven

Manning the grill, Jake nursed the last batch of burgers and sausages. His beans had been a huge success, as had Barrel's potato salad. The proof was in the four empty serving bowls soaking in the huge kitchen sink.

Everyone at Whistle Rock Ranch stood around talking or finishing their meal. Laughter was easy and ongoing. It had been a great evening. All felt right except for one factor.

Beth hadn't attended. Searching for her, he finally asked Virgil about the missing cook.

"Her mother?"

"Donna Jenner is one of the reasons we were able to hire Beth. Her mother still lives in Brilliance. Though she's not in the best of health."

"Serious?"

"It's complicated, Jake. When the time is right, ask Beth about her family. It's an interesting story." Forking a couple sausages off the grill, Virgil sauntered away as an SUV pulled into the ranch. Jake watched Beth get out, her face giving away nothing about the visit with her mother.

She stopped to talk to a few people on her way to the kitchen. Before she reached it, Jake stepped in front of her.

"Hey, Beth. How about a hamburger or a couple sausages?"

"Do you have any of your famous beans left?"

The grin disappeared. "Afraid not."

"No worries. I'm tired anyway. Thought I'd check the condition of the kitchen before heading to my cabin. Goodnight, Jake."

Setting down the spatula, he reached out his arm to stop her. "Don't go in there."

"It's pretty bad, huh?"

"Worse than that. Barrel and I will clean up before we sack out for the night."

"No need. I'll start washing now."

"Not a chance, Beth. Virgil said this is your night off. Go talk to people or head to your cabin. But you're not allowed in the kitchen."

Arching a brow, her mouth twisted into an almost grin. "Not allowed?"

"Yep."

"Who's going to stop me?"

He looked around, shrugging. "Me."

She wanted to challenge him, see what would happen. Her tired brain and body won out. "It has been a long day. So, if you're sure."

"I'm sure. Barrel will tell you the same."

They stared at each other for what seemed several minutes when only seconds had passed. Tearing her gaze away, she nodded.

"All right. Thanks, Jake. And thank Barrel for me." She waved an arm toward her cabin. "Goodnight."

"Goodnight, Beth."

His gaze followed her, hoping she'd glance back. She didn't.

Virgil gathered all the employees in the large barn the following morning. The old-timers knew what the topic would be, and relaxed while cradling cups of coffee. Though new to the ranch, Jake did the same. Others, such as Brady Blackwolf, were unsettled.

"For you new employees, we are not cutting staff, so you can relax." Virgil glanced at his cousin Brady, who released a pent-up breath. "What I'm going to say is important, so listen up. Margie and Anson Bonner invite their neighbors and townsfolk to Whistle Rock Ranch every Thanksgiving. This may not seem a big deal to a few of you. Those who've worked at the ranch for a while already know it's one of the biggest events of the year."

Virgil shot a look at Wyatt, who leaned against a stall, his arms crossed. "Last year, we had over two hundred people."

He let that sink in for a moment. "Nacho and Emma, the previous assistant cook, prepared a dozen large turkeys, ten hams, five legs of lamb, and six venison roasts. No burgers, hot dogs, or sausages. Along with the meat, there are endless appetizers, salads, vegetable dishes, and rolls."

"Are you asking us to help Beth cook, boss?"

Virgil grinned, waiting until the laughter died down. "Not a chance. We're bringing in people to help her. Everyone for miles knows this is a working ranch, and that doesn't change. Chores and other work goes on as usual. For Thanksgiving, we'll need to erect a couple of large tents, portable heaters, and several tables with chairs. We own the tents. The rest we rent. Depending on weather and how much snow is on the ground, we'll set everything up on Tuesday, Wednesday, and early Thursday. That will allow us to get our regular work done. Any questions so far?"

"I guess none of us should take time off around Thanksgiving." Jimmy chuckled.

"You'd be right. What else?"

"Is it still all right if we invite our families on Thanksgiving?" Owen Baker lived in a small house at the north edge of town with his wife and two children.

"Absolutely. No need for Marta to cook with the spread we'll have here."

"Girlfriends?"

"You mean some woman agreed to go out with you, Kenny?" Barrel's question had the men busting out with laughter while Kenny's face turned red.

"Definitely invite her," Virgil answered.

"What about teardown?"

"Depending on when everyone heads home, we might be able to start Thursday evening. Most times, we teardown on Friday. That's when the rental company picks up their stuff. What else?"

When no one else spoke up, Wyatt stepped forward. "This is a huge deal for my mother. She starts planning in September. If she pulls you aside to help with something, that becomes your first priority. Same with Pop, although he tends to stay in his office while we're working."

"If there are no other questions, get on with your chores." Virgil motioned for Jake to stay behind. "I'm picking up my parents at the airport on Thursday morning. You're going to need to take my place while I'm gone."

"No problem, boss. Seems to me a lot will depend on the weather. Will the tents hold up if there's a snowstorm?"

"To a point. They're made of heavy duty materials, but if we get a big dump on Thanksgiving, it'll be sketchy."

"Has it ever happened?"

"Three times that I remember," Virgil answered. "Two of those were before Margie started inviting everyone. The last one was maybe ten years ago. Everyone came inside. We opened Anson's and Margie's offices for people to spread out. Some ate in the kitchen. That was before we doubled the size for the guest ranch. There were maybe a hundred people that year. The thing is, if they call for a large storm, a lot of the people who may have planned to come will stay home. It could be a non-event."

"It'll work out. We won't let Margie down."

"I know you won't, Jake."

The days passed with a few days of moderate snow, though nothing ominous. Jake continued to take on more responsibilities, resulting in him falling into bed late and rising early.

Jake thought he knew a good deal about running a ranch and managing ranch hands. Working alongside Virgil illustrated how much he still had to learn.

There'd been no additional sightings of the wild dog pack. The search organized by the game and fish department had turned up little. Old tracks and carcasses from months earlier, which could've been the result of coyotes, wolves, or wild dogs. Since no other attacks had been reported, the urgency to locate them faded.

He'd seen little of Beth other than when she set out food for meals. Jake tried to ignore how much not talking to her bothered him.

Spending time figuring out why took more emotional effort than this cowboy was willing to spend. Yet he thought about her several times each day, and as he fell asleep at night.

"Morning, Jake." Virgil strolled up, holding two cups of coffee. "Do you have a few minutes to talk?"

Nodding, he took the cup Virgil held out. "What do you need?"

"The weather report is calling for mild weather for Thanksgiving. It's Monday now, so I'm considering starting the set-up tomorrow. One tent tomorrow and the other on Wednesday. Tables and chairs will be delivered Wednesday afternoon. They won't take much time to place inside the tents. Anything stopping us from starting tomorrow?"

"Nope. We're caught up." Taking a sip of coffee, Jake looked past Virgil to the large barn. "The truth is, the boys need something to do."

"We have at least three more men than needed right now. When the guest ranch reopens, we will need them. Wyatt and I ran the numbers on letting them go and finding replacements in the spring versus keeping them on. The three I'm thinking of are great workers, the guests loved them, and they're solid wranglers."

"What'd you find?"

"It cost more to keep them on," Vigil answered. "Though the difference was negligible. So small we decided not to make any changes. We'll start building additional cabins in March. Guests start arriving in mid-June. Having the same crew as last year will streamline the process."

"Understandable. How many new cabins?"

"Seven. That accounts for adding replacements for the cabins you and Beth are using. We'll net five new ones." Tossing out the last bit of his coffee, Virgil shifted toward the house. "There is one other issue. Nacho may not return."

"I see. Does Beth know?"

"Not yet. We want her to take over Nacho's position. Wyatt said you might know someone who'd be interested in working as her assistant."

Jake knew Wyatt meant Helena. She'd trained as a chef, worked for large ranching operations. When mentioning her to Wyatt, he'd felt confident she'd be sober by now. The hope had shattered with her last phone call.

"She won't work out, Virgil. I do know another person who might be perfect. No experience cooking on a ranch, but Beth is so solid, I don't see that being an issue."

"Availability?"

"I'll have to call her."

"Do it, Jake. The sooner we identify someone, the better."

Nodding, he shifted from one foot to the other. "There is something you need to know about her."

Lifting a brow, Virgil cocked his head to the side. "Tell me."

"She's my older sister."

Chapter Eight

Margie kept Beth busy planning for Thanksgiving. From meals to the layout of tables and chairs inside the tents, they discussed every detail. Jake entered the kitchen as the women were taking a break.

"Jake." Margie walked toward him, touching his arm. "How nice to see you. Wyatt told me you were in charge of the tents and outdoor set-up for Thanksgiving."

Removing his hat, a grin curved his lips. "Yes, ma'am. If the weather cooperates, we'll erect the first tent tomorrow. The second on Wednesday." He shot a look at Beth. "I need to know where you want them placed."

"Good idea. Beth, you should come with us."

"All right."

Instead of heading toward the side of the lodge with the barn, Margie walked to the other side. Big trees dotted what Jake guessed to be about an acre.

"One will go right here, between these trees. The other will go over there." She indicated another open spot bordered by more trees. "Each has four sides that you'll stake down, and openings about eight feet wide that serve as entrances for guests. The openings should face each other. Six tables will fit in each tent, with eight guests each. So, almost a hundred people can be seated between the two tents. It works since we serve food between one and five in the afternoon."

"Will there be any tables available inside the lodge?" Beth asked.

"A few for older people and those who require assistance." Margie tapped her lips. "Last year, we used four tables. We now have the six tables purchased for the guest ranch visitors. Using those would be best." She directed the last at Jake.

"Yes, ma'am."

Margie began walking back to the lodge. "I'll be here tomorrow if you have questions. If the weather is good, you might want to erect both."

"Virgil doesn't want to take the men away from their normal work for long. With this being my first year setting this up, I'd better check with him."

Margie stopped at the steps to the lodge. "Of course. Do whatever you think is best. Beth, I need to make some phone calls."

"No problem. I think we've covered everything. I have some food to prep for Thursday." Beth gave a small wave at Margie and Jake before walking up the steps.

"Beth, do you have a few minutes?"

Turning, she faced Jake. "A couple. Let's go inside." She didn't stop until entering the kitchen. He watched as she placed three large sheet pans filled with brownie dough into the large, industrial oven.

"Are those what you use for us?"

Closing the oven doors, she chuckled. "I use one for our dinners. There are usually cookies and sometimes a few pies. Thanksgiving falls into its own category. I've already made and frozen three pans of brownies and ten dozen cookies. I'll make three kinds of pies tomorrow and Wednesday. Pumpkin, pecan, and apple. So, what did you want to talk about?"

"Virgil said he talked to you this morning about the possibility Nacho might not return."

Her features fell as her shoulders slumped. "Yes. I'd hoped to have more time with him. He's an amazing cook."

"Virgil told me the odds of him returning are maybe thirty percent."

Beth leaned against the counter, crossing her arms. "I'd say twenty, tops."

"Assuming he doesn't return, Virgil asked if I knew of someone who'd be interested in working as your assistant."

Her eyes lit up. "Do you have someone?"

"Maybe. She's not a professional chef."

"That's all right. I can train her."

Setting his hat on the counter, he shoved both hands in his pockets. "She has a certificate in culinary arts. Her experience is limited to family restaurants and small hotels. Sometimes, when they were low on staff, she'd waitress and cook."

"I did the same when attending university. It was good experience. Do you think she would be interested in working on a ranch?"

"The thing is, she lost her job a month ago when the restaurant closed. No severance, so she had to move out of her apartment. The economy is down and jobs are scarce."

"Where'd she go?"

"That's the thing, Beth. She moved in with our aunt. Abigail is my older sister."

"Really? This calls for talking over coffee." She pointed to a small table with two chairs in a corner. "Cream, sugar?"

"A little cream. Milk is fine too." Watching as she prepared coffee, he relaxed, glad she hadn't shot down the idea of hiring Abigail.

Setting the cups on the table, she removed the brownie pans from the oven before sitting down. "So, tell me about your older sister."

Jake cradled the coffee cup, taking the occasional sip as he spoke. He finished at the same time as his last swallow of the excellent brew. Abigail had asked him to stick to her experience and not bring up her personal life unless he had to.

"That's what I know about her schooling and experience."

Beth leaned back, staring into her cooling coffee. "Sounds as if she'd work out real well here. Would she need space for a husband or children?"

"No on both."

"And you've already talked to her?"

"Early this morning. She's real interested. Would you like her number? Might be best if you spoke to her directly." He pulled his phone from a pocket.

"I'll need to call today. The rest of the week is going to be crazy."

Reading off Abigail's number, he slid the phone away. "Thanks, Beth. I hope this works out for both of you." Standing, he set his cup in the sink.

"Another question, Jake. Do you have any issue having your sister here on the ranch?"

"None at all. I'm only a year younger. We were real close growing up. It would be great to have her here."

"I'll talk to Virgil about salary and other details, then call her. Thanks, Jake. This is great." She held up the small piece of paper with Abigail's number.

"Glad to help." He moved to the back door, where his feet stalled. Several seconds ticked by before he turned the knob and stepped outside.

Grumbling, he took one quick glance behind him. Beth stood at the window. She could've been looking out at anything. Jake would've laid odds her gaze tracked him on the way to the barn.

It took little time to tack up Cisco. Glad to put distance between him and Beth, he headed out. Taking a truck might have been faster. The pleasure gained from riding helped clear his head, tugging him back from a dangerous precipice. What was the woman doing to him?

Spending time with Beth did nothing to support his determination to give rodeoing another try. She intrigued him, ruling his thoughts day and night. He found himself looking for her around the ranch, knowing she'd be in the kitchen. Nothing in his life made much sense, especially not the irrational desire to be near her. Determined to regain control of his errant feelings, he followed the tire tracks to join the other ranch hands.

The men had hauled hay to the cattle, weeks earlier than the previous year. If the snow continued to hinder normal grazing into January, they'd haul protein tubs out to bulk up the cattle in preparation for calving season. Both actions were costly, eating into the ranch's profits. The ranch's ability to grow enough hay for their own use helped keep costs down.

He met them as they returned. Four men and an empty truck bed and trailer. Jimmy stopped and leaned out the window.

"We're finished, Jake. If the weather holds, the snow may melt enough for them to graze before the next storm." He glanced up to the sky. "Out of our hands and into God's."

"It's the way of it, Jimmy. I'll meet you back at the barn after taking a look around."

"We saw no sign of the wild dogs."

"I'm still going to check again for tracks. They're somewhere not far away. I can feel it."

Giving a slow nod, Jimmy continued on while Jake rode west.

He'd woken that morning with the dog pack on his mind. Odd, yet not unfamiliar.

The same used to happen when he faced tough competition during his rodeo days. An itching sensation would follow him during the day, the same as this morning.

Reaching down, he touched his rifle. On the other side of the saddle, his shotgun lay cradled in its scabbard. The gunbelt his father had given him held a .45 caliber six-shooter. Another gift from his father.

He'd ridden another thirty minutes before deciding to turn around. Reining Cisco toward the barn, he stilled at an unmistakable growl.

Drawing the shotgun from its sheath, he brought a dancing Cisco under control. Another growl had him reeling the horse around to face a dense stand of trees and thick bushes. To his back was open range. The same on his right and left. Nothing ominous in those directions. The noise had to have come from right in front of him.

Staying watchful, he signaled Cisco to back up. Jake didn't want to confront whatever stood hidden out there. He'd hoped to determine if it was the dog pack or wolves. His answer came seconds later.

Two dogs approached from the bushes to his right as three dogs loomed straight ahead. At first, he saw nothing to his left. Then a dreadfully thin dog stepped forward several feet to the left of those in front of him. Six dogs growled as they moved toward him.

Cisco continued to dance around, fear in his deep brown eyes. Jake's calm, soothing voice helped to settle the gelding. It would prove temporary.

Raising the shotgun, he aimed at the three dogs centered in front of him. He'd get at least one—more if they stayed in a tight group.

Teeth bared, the six dogs advanced on some silent signal. Focusing on the dog in the middle, he let out a breath, began to slap the trigger when a gunshot came from his right.

Confused, his shot went high when Cisco bucked. Staying in the saddle, he reined the gelding around. It was then he noticed one of the dogs on the ground. The others had scattered, leaving their comrade behind as they disappeared into the woods.

Jake recognized the figure riding toward him. Virgil still held the rifle in one hand, his long, black ponytail waving in the air as he rode forward. The sight reminded Jake of the foreman's Northern Cheyenne heritage.

"Where did you come from?" Jake slipped his shotgun away.

"Jimmy told me you'd continued on alone to look for tracks. Not a good idea, Jake."

Under normal circumstances, he'd give a sharp retort. The reality was Virgil may have saved his life.

"Stupid move. I wasn't expecting to come across the whole pack. From now on, I'll get someone to ride with me."

"Good idea." Virgil slipped to the ground, closing the distance between him and the downed animal. He found no pulse.

"Any sign of rabies?"

Virgil shook his head. "No, but I want to take him back and have the doc make a determination. He's small, which is good."

Jake helped wrap the animal in a blanket and tie him in front of Virgil. As the men swung into their saddles, a chorus of mournful howls cut through the air. A reminder they still weren't alone.

Chapter Nine

"Jimmy, do you have that corner?" Jake held his spot while Barrel, Jimmy, and Owen did the same at the other three corners. They'd already put in a full day before tackling the first tent.

"I'm set, Jake."

"All right. Let's tie this thing down." He nodded at a ranch hand standing a few feet away.

While the man moved from corner to corner, Jake and the others checked the side panels. They'd be tied up tonight so wind could move through the tent without creating damage.

Done for the day, the others headed to the bunkhouse while Jake walked to his cabin. Taking a quick shower, he dressed in clean clothes, checked himself in the mirror, and headed straight to the kitchen. He stepped inside without knocking.

The room buzzed with activity. Owen's wife, Marta, assembled pies alongside a woman he didn't recognize. Another woman he'd never met prepared homemade yeast rolls. Beth stood across the room, preparing a ham for baking. Finished, she set it next to the rest of the meat inside one of two giant commercial refrigerators. Turning, she spotted him for the first time.

"Jake. When did you get here?"

He walked toward her as if drawn by some invisible force. "A few minutes ago. Lots going on in here."

"We still have more to do before guests arrive on Thanksgiving."

"I see you pulled in Owen's wife." He nodded toward the pretty, petite woman a few feet away.

"She's a gem and a great cook. If you hadn't found Abigail for us, I may have tried to talk Marta into helping us out on a temporary basis. Did you know she works mornings at Daisy's shop?"

"Owen never mentioned her having a job. I know they have a couple kids."

"A boy, Cory, and girl, Janie. Cory and Koa are good friends. Marta told me Cory might go to Trace's ranch for a few days at Christmas so the boys can spend time together."

"You know, I did hear something about that when I spoke to Trace last week."

Beth's eyes widened. "That's right. You and Trace are best friends. He recommended you to take over for him."

"Yep."

"So what brought you in here before dinner?"

"I, uh, stopped in to see if you needed anything from me or the men before Thursday." It wasn't the complete truth. More than anything, Jake had wanted to spend a few minutes with Beth before joining the others in the dining room for taco Tuesday.

Clasping her hands together, she made a slow turn, pressing her lips together. "You're already doing so much."

"The tents, tables, and chairs don't take much time. If there's anything else..."

"Well, I am a little concerned about getting the food from the kitchen to the buffet tables in the lodge and those in the tents."

"I didn't realize there'd be buffet tables in the tents. Good information."

"According to Margie, there were a few problems in previous years with guests filling their plates inside, then spilling them on the way to the tents. She changed the way food is served about five years ago. Since then, there have been very few problems."

"We'll set up the buffet tables with the rest of the tables. When the food is ready, I'll have three men available to carry the serving plates out of the kitchen."

She gave him an impish smile, which did nothing to cool his interest in her. "Will you be one of those men?"

He returned her grin. "Absolutely."

"Your help would be appreciated. People start arriving around twelve-thirty. We serve food between one and five. Margie says it's best putting the food out right at one o'clock."

"We'll be here a little before then and stick around until everyone's been served. Will that work?"

"I'm thinking of putting the last of the food out between four and four-thirty. If you arrive at twelve, there'll be time for you and your men to eat before setting out food for the guests. What do you think?"

"You sure we won't be in your way, Beth?"

"I'm certain. I'd better get back to preparing more food. If you're hungry, taco fixings are already set out in the dining room."

"That's where I'm headed." He continued to stand next to her a few more seconds before forcing himself to move.

"Jake?"

Turning to see Beth already at one of the prep areas, he stopped. "Yeah?"

"Thanks."

Jake filled his plate with three beef tacos, three chicken tacos, rice, beans, guacamole dip, and chips. Finding a chair next to Virgil, he filled his glass with ice water from one of three pitchers on the table. Digging in, he hummed in satisfaction.

"No one makes better tacos," he said to no one in particular.

Virgil took several swallows of water before setting his glass down. "Nacho was wise to use her recipe."

"Sure was. His were good." Jake held up a taco. "Beth's are great."

Virgil let him get halfway through his meal before speaking again. "The wild dog I shot was infected with rabies."

The comment caused Jake to pause with a forkful of rice partway to his mouth. He set it down. "Didn't show any signs."

"I know. Still, the tests are positive. Doc Worrel notified our area's warden. He called this morning. I'll be driving him out to where we spotted them. Do you want to ride along?"

"When?"

"Tomorrow morning at nine." Virgil scooped up the last bite of black beans.

"Should be fine." Picking up his last taco, he set it down, his appetite waning. "The fact they're still so close to the lodge isn't good."

"I know."

"It's because the entire pack is infected with rabies." Downing the last of his water, Jake sat back.

"That's my guess. Wish I'd gotten a better look at the others before shooting. 'Course, that would've meant leaving you vulnerable."

A bland chuckle escaped Jake's lips. "You made the right choice."

"Probably." Virgil shoved his chair back. "The warden will want to organize another search."

"I figured as much. When?"

Shrugging, Virgil stood. "He won't want to interrupt Thanksgiving. Friday's my guess. Saturday at the latest."

"The sooner the better. It's unsettling to have a rabid pack so close to the lodge." Standing, he walked with Virgil to a tub where they set down their plates and utensils.

"They're a threat I want to eliminate as soon as we can." Settling his hat on his head, Virgil sauntered off.

Beth walked toward her cabin, deciding thirty minutes to rejuvenate would be time well spent. In three hours, she'd have tonight's dinner ready for the ranch hands. While they ate, she'd bake the last pans of brownies and chocolate chip cookies.

Trying not to appear obvious, she searched the area for Jake. She'd seen him and Virgil talk during lunch, suspecting the topic might have been the pack of wild dogs.

Everyone whispered about the rabid animals, their voices ranging from curiosity to dread. Beth had heard stories of wild packs attacking cattle, horses, and the occasional human. They hunted for food during the day, returning to their dens at night.

The difference was the pack patrolling the area around Whistle Rock Ranch were rabid. Animals carrying the deadly sickness weren't rational. Rabies ravaged their brains. Instead of hunting deer or domestic animals, they acted irrationally, and were more apt to attack a person.

The sound of cheering from the other side of the barn had her making a detour. Rounding one side, she stopped at the sight ahead of her.

Two of the ranch hands, Jimmy and Kenny, rolled on the ground, their fists flying. What surprised her was to see

Virgil, Wyatt, and Jake standing off to the side. They weren't shouting like the others, yet they made no move to stop the fighting.

She'd never witnessed an actual fight. Shoving and pushing, yes, but never two men locked in a battle that could cause permanent damage. Making up her mind to stop the two young men, she took a step closer. A strong hand wrapped around her arm to pull her close.

"They'll be fine, Beth. They're just releasing some of their frustration."

"Those boys could hurt each other, Jake."

"Jimmy and Kenny aren't boys. They're men who've proven their worth on the ranch."

Her gaze never wavered from the two ranch hands. "Why are they fighting?"

"I wasn't there when it started, but Virgil believes it has something to do with a certain young woman. Seems both want to invite her to Thanksgiving dinner."

"Ah." A grin split her face. "Why don't they both sit with her?"

"Guess you don't have much experience with two men vying for your attention."

Before Beth could respond, Virgil and Wyatt grabbed the arms of the young men, pulling them apart. Slapping them on their backs, they ordered Jimmy and Kenny to shake hands before sending them away to clean up.

"Each day on the ranch brings something new." She watched the young men stumble away, shaking her head.

"Growing up in town is different from being on a ranch. At the same time, much is the same."

She raised a brow. "Such as?"

"Human feelings. Joy, anger, frustration, elation. Everyone experiences them, no matter where they grow up. When was the first time you rode a horse?"

She thought back to high school. "Sixteen. A girlfriend's family owned a ranch south of Brilliance. She invited me out to ride. My mother said no, but my father, well…he said I could go. I'm sure they had words about it later."

"Did you enjoy riding?"

Glancing at the ground, she allowed herself a moment to reminisce. "It was wonderful."

He took a step closer. "Then you and I will have to ride sometime soon."

Chapter Ten

Beth didn't return to her cabin. Jake's invitation had taken her by surprise, erasing the plans she had for relaxing in her cabin.

Telling herself his comment meant little, she went back to work. The snow had come early and would continue through February, possibly March. Riding would be difficult if not impossible, at least for a rider with little experience, such as herself.

The roasts she'd placed in the oven at a low temperature still had a couple hours to go. Perfect timing for Beth to prepare red skinned potatoes for roasting.

Chopping the fresh rosemary grown in the ranch's garden, she heard the back door open. Not taking the time to look up, she continued her work.

"I'm looking for Beth."

"You've found her."

"I'm Abigail Kelman."

Beth's head snapped up to see a beautiful woman with short brown hair and caramel brown eyes. Her slender form and olive complexion reminded Beth of Abigail's younger brother, Jake.

Wiping her hands down her apron, she smiled. "I'm so glad to meet you. I wasn't expecting you so soon."

Abigail shuffled from one foot to the other, her features wary. "I hope it's all right I came early."

"Absolutely. Thanksgiving for so many takes a lot of work. I hope you're prepared for a few long days."

Relaxing, her features softened. "I am. Tell me what you need done and I'll start right now."

"Have you seen Jake?"

"Not yet. I thought it was more important to let you know I'd arrived."

"First things first. You'll be staying in an apartment behind the kitchen. I imagine you have some luggage in your car."

"It's right outside. I, um...rode the bus to Brilliance. An older rancher was coming this way and offered to drop me off."

"Well, let's get your luggage to the apartment, then we'll find Jake. I know he'll be glad to see you." Opening the back door, Beth grabbed two of three bags. The ones she picked up were held together with duct tape. The third wasn't in much better condition.

"The last assistant cook lived back here with her son. Very cozy." Opening the door, she entered, setting the bags on the sofa. She swept her arm in the air. "Living room, efficiency kitchen, bedroom, and bathroom. You're always welcome to use the kitchen up front."

"It's more than I imagined." Abigail placed the third bag on the floor.

"I'll get you a key. Ready to find your brother?"

"Um, sure."

Beth frowned at the lack of enthusiasm in Abigail's voice. She'd expected her to be excited to see Jake. He was, after all, the reason Abigail had been offered the job.

"He could be anywhere. We'll check the barn and corrals first."

Abigail didn't respond as she followed Beth into the cold. Glancing over her shoulder at her new assistant, she focused on the frayed, well-worn coat. Arms crossed to hold in the heat, Abigail shivered as the wind whipped around them. They'd have to do something about the coat, but that was a topic for later.

Spotting Jimmy, Beth kept her mouth shut when she noticed the bruising on his face. "Do you know where Jake is?"

Jimmy's attention landed on Abigail as he formed an answer. "He's working with a new horse in the corral closest to the barn." He touched the brim of his hat, his gaze never leaving the unfamiliar woman. "I'm Jimmy, ma'am."

"Sorry. This is Abigail, Jake's sister."

"Nice to meet you, ma'am."

"Nice to meet you, too." Her response lacked the warmth expected.

"Thanks, Jimmy. We'll go catch him before he disappears." Beth continued around the barn. A few ranch hands stood outside the corral, watching as Jake worked with the young horse.

"Afternoon, Barrel."

Turning, he tore off his hat. "Hey, Beth. Jake's working with a green horse. He's real good at calming them." He nodded toward the corral. "This one's going to go for a lot of money when he's through with him."

"A gelding?"

"Yes, ma'am."

"Abigail, this is Jeramy Barrel. Barrel, this is Abigail Kelman, Jake's sister."

His eyes widened, indicating his surprise. "Real pleasure to meet you, ma'am."

"Mr. Barrel."

Smiling, he settled his hat back on his head. "No Mr., just Barrel."

Abigail didn't respond, choosing to move into an open spot along the fence to watch Jake. Beth noticed her features didn't change as he worked with the young gelding. They were as placid as when she'd introduced herself in the kitchen.

Jake held out his hand, taking a blanket from Brady. Letting the gelding smell it, he slid it over his neck and withers before setting it on his back.

"Will he saddle him now?" Beth asked.

"No." Abigail answered before Barrel had a chance. "Jake will make sure the horse is comfortable with the blanket before setting a saddle on him. It's a process he's used for as long as I can remember."

Jake finished about fifteen minutes later, handing the gelding's lead line to Brady. Walking to the gate, he lifted his gaze, a smile forming when he spotted Beth. His attention moved to the woman next to her.

"Abbie!" Rushing to her, he wrapped both arms around her, swinging her in a circle.

Laughing, she lightly slapped him on the back. "Let me down."

Doing as she asked, he kissed her cheek. "I didn't know you'd be here so soon. This is great. Obviously, you've met Beth."

"And Jimmy and Barrel." Her smile slipped just a little. "Beth showed me the apartment. It's very nice." She was thankful he'd never seen her last apartment. According to a girlfriend, it was an affordable dump. Abigail had done all she could to make it comfortable before her life fell apart.

"I'm so glad you're here, Ab." He drew her into another hug. "I have work to finish. Let's talk after dinner."

Kissing his cheek, she stepped back, forcing away a tear threatening to fall. "Sounds good."

Frowning, he studied her face. "Are you all right?"

Forcing a smile, she squeezed his arm. "I'm great. Now, go on and do your thing."

Jake looked as if he wanted to say something more before shaking his head and walking toward the barn.

"Are you ready to help me with dinner or do you need time to rest?"

Tearing her attention from Jake's retreating back, she turned toward Beth. "I'm definitely ready to work."

Beth's phone vibrated at the exact moment the oven alarm signaled the roasts were done. Ignoring the phone, she slid them out of the oven and onto the counter.

"Abigail, can you check the potatoes and baked chickens in the other oven?"

"Sure." Removing the potatoes from the oven, she covered them with foil. "The chicken needs a little more time. I'll check them in a few minutes."

Tossing sliced tomatoes into two large salad bowls, she groaned when her phone rang again. This time, she answered, tucking the phone between her shoulder and ear.

"Hello." She grimaced an instant later, realizing it was another call from the same person who'd been harassing her. Refusing to listen to the electronically modified voice, she ended the call. Sighing, she stared at the floor before returning her attention to the unfinished salads.

"Everything all right, Beth?"

"What? Oh, yes. Everything's fine," she lied.

The caller never gave her a clue as to why he was stalking her. The point of each call centered on how she'd be sorry for the injustice of her family. It made no sense. She wasn't married, didn't have a boyfriend. Her oldest brother was married, running a successful business. The next oldest, Thomas, had earned an MBA, and now held a controller position with a large company. As far as Beth knew, he was still a carefree bachelor.

She'd considered calling Julian and Thomas to see if either had experienced the same harassing calls. Beth disregarded the idea each time, knowing her brothers would think she was overreacting. Maybe she was.

"This too will pass." She muttered the words under her breath, hoping they were true.

"The French bread is ready to serve. I've put the loaves in the warming oven."

Beth glanced up, forgetting Abigail stood a few feet away. "Thank you. Starving workers should be coming through the dining room doors any minute. Do you know how to carve the meat?"

"I've done it many times."

"Great. You can place the slices on platters over there." She nodded toward a table holding several serving bowls and platters. "The potatoes can go into the large bowls. The chicken should be placed on the other platter. The vegetable casseroles may be served as is. The French bread should be placed in the fabric lined basket."

It wasn't long before the sound of people talking and laughing while piling food onto plates wafted into the kitchen. The women prepared several more platters and bowls to replace the empty ones in the dining room. They wouldn't be able to relax until dessert had been served. Even then, a ten minute coffee break would be all they could take before clearing and cleaning the buffet table.

Beth couldn't get the latest phone call out of her head. Adding it to the others over the last few weeks, she estimated almost a dozen crank calls. They were as frustrating as they were unsettling.

An electronically modified voice always started with a greeting, as if they were old friends. The following sentences hinted at wrongdoing by her family and how the caller would make them pay for their misdeeds. Nothing too blatant. Nothing she could take to the authorities or share with her brothers. The perfect method of intimidation without a direct threat.

Beth knew the obvious way to handle future calls was not to answer. If she didn't recognize the number, it would go to voicemail. It didn't take much imagination to know the caller would hang up rather than leave a message.

After a while, the caller would give up and move on to some other unfortunate person. Probably another woman.

Walking to her cabin, she shivered as the chill worked its way through her coat and blouse. Stepping inside, the dark interior reinforced how alone she felt. Thinking about the events of the last few months contributed to her loneliness.

People she believed were friends in Jackson had disappeared with the loss of her relationship with the resort owner. Numerous harassing phone calls from an unknown person served to increase her sense of isolation.

Lowering herself into one of two chairs, she stared into the cabin's darkness, in no hurry to turn on a light. There were times when a woman needed to wallow in melancholy, if only for a while. Tonight seemed destined to be one of those times.

A knock on the door interfered with her glum mood. Flipping on a light, she looked through the peephole. Confused, she opened the door.

"Jake. What are you doing here?"

He motioned toward the kitchen. "I just left Abigail's apartment and am not quite ready to head back to my cabin. Any interest in taking a walk?" He held out a hand.

Chapter Eleven

Beth had thought to beg off, saying she had some work to do. The look in Jake's eyes, the waiting open hand, had her reaching out.

His was a warm, weathered hand, and felt reassuring and protective. A strange thought, Beth mused. When several feet from the cabin, she lightly tugged her hand, intending to pull it from his. He held on.

"Not yet."

She allowed herself a smile. "It is a beautiful night. I'm glad you thought of me."

"What were you doing before I arrived?"

Beth considered what she should say. *Feeling sorry for myself,* didn't sound right. "Not much. Unwinding from another crazy day."

Guiding her toward the barn, he fell silent until they were inside. "What do you think of Abigail?"

"She's a hard worker. Wherever she's worked before trained her well. I'm lucky to have her. What are we doing in the barn?"

"Checking on my horse. He favored one leg today, which isn't normal." Stopping at a stall, he drew Beth next to him. "This is Cisco, my quarter horse gelding."

"My gosh, he's gorgeous."

"He's a sorrel, with what most think is a black mane and tail."

"They aren't black?"

"They're actually an extremely dark shade of red, which appears black against his red coat. I've had him since birth. He's been my partner for a long time."

Dropping her hand, he slid the halter and lead line from a hook. "I'm going to walk him around for a bit. Let me know if you think he's limping."

Beth almost protested about her lack of knowledge, but let it go. Surely, she could tell if a horse limped or not.

She watched, fascinated at how easily the horse slipped into his halter. "Cisco, my man, let's get you out of here."

Beth spotted a slight limp the instant Jake led him from the stall. "He's favoring his left hind leg."

"I thought so." He guided Cisco in a circle, turning him toward the stall. Removing the halter, he left him long enough to retrieve a bottle of Bigeloil. Squeezing some in his hands, he rubbed it into the sore leg before wrapping it.

Standing, he looked over at Beth. "I'll take the wrap off in the morning and check him again. I doubt it's serious, but you never know."

"He's a beauty, Jake."

"Thanks." Picking up her hand, he continued out the other end of the barn. She didn't try to tug her hand away this time.

"The horse you worked with today will be sold?"

"I don't know what Wyatt has in mind. Virgil mentioned they may already have a buyer. He's a gelding, so my guess is he'll be used as a cow pony or general riding. He seems to have the conformation and temperament to compete in Western or English events. Might make a good cutting horse, though I doubt that's the way Wyatt or Virgil would go."

"Why's that?"

"It's not what they do here. Barrel racing, maybe. Cutting horses generally have a short competition period before they're retired. But, hey, it's not my call. My job is to move him out of being a green broke horse and get him used to a saddle. He's real smart. I doubt it will take long."

They continued walking as light flecks of snow floated around them. Beth reached out her free hand to catch a few flakes. "I sure hope we don't get a storm coming through on Thanksgiving. We'll never fit all those people inside the lodge."

"It's supposed to be clear."

"Things in Wyoming can change in a heartbeat."

Jake chuckled. "As well I know. If one does come through, the odds are most of the people won't show up."

"We'd end up with a crazy amount of food. Margie is already sending enough meals for a hundred people to the local shelter. They'll get a lot more than that if a storm comes our way."

Jake led them in a huge circle around the bunkhouse, corrals, and cabins before stopping at hers. Releasing her hand, he stroked a finger down her arm.

"Thanks for coming with me, Beth."

"Anytime you want company on your walk, you know where I'll be."

A grin tipped up the corners of his mouth. "Good to know. I'll see you tomorrow, Beth. Sleep well."

"You too, Jake."

Waiting until she closed the door behind her, he walked the short distance to his cabin, feeling just a little lighter.

Waking to the sun slicing through the curtains, Beth threw off the covers. Rubbing her eyes, her mouth curved into a smile. The walk with Jake had been just the medicine she'd needed to shake off the melancholy of the previous night.

Stretching both arms above her head, she made the mistake of glancing at the clock.

"Oh, no!" She'd overslept by almost an hour.

Rushing to wash up and dress, she stuffed her feet into work boots and all but ran to the kitchen. Shoving the door open, she stepped inside, stopping at what she saw.

Abigail stood at the work counter mixing batter for pancakes. She could smell cooked bacon, and spotted a bowl of cracked eggs ready to be scrambled.

Slipping out of her coat, she moved closer to Abigail. "How did you know what to do?"

Her assistant pointed to the whiteboard on the far wall. "You spelled it out for me."

Beth had forgotten about her penchant to write down menus at least two days in advance. "I'm so glad you took the initiative to start without me. Thank you."

"No problem. This is the type of cooking I've done for a long time. Do you think I've made enough?" She walked to the warmer where pans of cooked bacon and sausages were covered with foil. Pulling back the foil, she stood aside so Beth could see. "What do you think?"

"We might need a little more bacon. The amount of sausages is perfect."

"There are four pans of muffins in the ovens. They should be ready in about ten minutes. I've finished the pancake batter. Do you cook them and put them in the warming oven, or wait?"

"Cook and keep them warm." Beth checked the time. "They'll be arriving any minute." As the words left her mouth, the sound of boots on the wood floor and people talking came from the dining room.

"Coffee, tea, and water are all set up," Abigail said. "I'll take the bacon and sausages out with the muffins."

"I'll cook the eggs and pancakes. First, I should let the men know we're running a bit late."

"I can do that, Beth. I'll blame it on me being new." When Beth tried to protest, Abigail waved her off. "No worries. It makes sense, and they won't think anything of it."

An hour later, when the employees had filled their stomachs, gone through gallons of coffee and dozens of muffins, Beth acknowledged Abigail was right.

She'd been surprised when several of the men, including Jake, had passed through the kitchen to thank them for a great breakfast. The actions had meant a lot to the women.

Beth noticed Jake lingered longer than necessary, watching his sister. Abigail didn't seem to notice his frown before he nodded at Beth and left.

Worry about his sister nagged at Jake. Abigail hadn't smiled since he'd picked her up and swung her in a circle when she'd arrived. What bothered him the most was how unusually quiet she'd been when he'd stopped by to talk the evening before.

The smiling, upbeat, always animated sister he'd expected had been quiet, seeming to draw within herself. She hadn't met his gaze the entire time he'd been inside her apartment. It wasn't a stretch to know something serious had happened besides losing her job. Given space, she might open up to him.

"Abigail sure is a nice lady, Jake. A good cook, too."

Setting down the last hoof of a newly shod horse, he pinned Jimmy with a glare, which had the young ranch hand taking a step back. "Other than thanking her for the food, I'd appreciate it if you'd stay away from her."

Jimmy held up his hands, palms out. "Sure, Jake. Whatever you say. I, uh...should get back to helping Virgil."

"Good idea." Jake hid a grin at the fear on the young man's face.

Closing the stall door, he headed toward Cisco. He'd wrapped the gelding's leg a second night. The limp had receded some, but not as much as he'd hoped. If he wasn't significantly better tomorrow, he'd call Doc Worrel.

Walking out of the barn into a clear day, he and several others would be erecting the second tent after lunch, before taking care of anything else Beth needed.

The weather report still insisted Thanksgiving would be free of storms. Glancing up at the sky, he wasn't so sure.

Spotting Virgil standing with a group of ranch hands about fifty yards away, he started toward them when his phone rang. Opening a pocket, his fingers fumbled with it before answering.

"Kelman."

"Hello, Jake."

Steps slowing, he let out a deep sigh while turning away from the group of men. "I'm real busy, Helena."

"I'm thinking of visiting you for Thanksgiving."

"Not a good idea."

"My parents left for Salt Lake City. Dad has relatives there. So, I don't have anyone here, Jake."

"I don't know what to tell you, Helena. I'm working all day tomorrow. The fact is, I don't foresee a day off until, well, maybe late next week. You've got other friends up there. Why don't you call them?"

"It's not the same as spending time with you."

Rubbing a hand over his forehead, he searched for the right words. "Listen to me, Helena. You need to focus on yourself, staying sober and finding work."

"Why can't I do those with you?"

"I tried helping you, and it didn't turn out so well. What about your cousin? She's still close by, right?"

"You know what, Jake? Just forget it. Like everything else in my life, I can do this on my own. I don't need you. I don't need anyone, and certainly not you." Her angry voice rose with each sentence. "Enjoy your turkey."

She ended the call before he could respond. "Just as well," he muttered, sliding the phone back into a pocket. Feeling sick, he sucked in a deep breath, holding it a few seconds before exhaling.

Being friends with Helena had always been a challenge. At one point, he wanted their relationship to be more. Looking at their lives now, he realized her addiction would've destroyed anything more than the fragile friendship they clung to.

Heading back toward Virgil, he hoped Helena found a place to enjoy Thanksgiving. He wasn't too worried. Even with her issues, she always found a way to land on her feet.

Chapter Twelve

"Beth. Can you bring out some of those fabulous cookies?"

"Sure, Mom." Removing the lid from the airtight container, she lifted several of her coconut, chocolate chip, and cashew cookies, placing them on a plate.

She'd driven to her mother's home in town to pick her up for tomorrow's Thanksgiving meal. Instead of her overnight bag being packed and ready to go, Beth found her entertaining Braydon Stiles.

Shy and prone to introspection, they'd been a year or two apart in high school. He'd attended college, and now headed a financial planning firm whose clients included Anson and Margie Bonner, and most of the large landowners, plus the mayor and numerous doctors. She had no idea why he thought her mother could afford his services, but kept the thought to herself.

"Here you are. More coffee, Braydon?"

"No, thank you. I won't be staying long." He grabbed another cookie. "These are fabulous, Beth."

"He came by to go over my account. It's doing very well, Beth."

She sat down next to her mother. "Since when did you have enough money to invest, Mom?"

Donna smiled at Braydon. "Oh, I've been saving a little bit from every paycheck since before your father died. I asked Braydon to handle my money a few years ago. It was small compared to his other clients, but he didn't turn me away."

"I'd never turn you away, Mrs. Jenner. Besides, your savings were well beyond the normal minimum."

"It's all worked out very well, Braydon."

"I should be going. April is making brunch, then we'll be going to Whistle Rock Ranch for Thanksgiving. I'll see you both there."

Beth stood. "I'll walk you out." Grabbing her coat, she slipped it on as they stepped outside. "Mother really did have more than your minimum?"

"Not a lot more, but yes. It's grown substantially, Beth. Your mother is a sharp woman."

"Wow. I had no idea she'd been putting money away. Makes me wonder what else I don't know about her. See you and April at Thanksgiving dinner."

"We're looking forward to it." Climbing into a new metallic silver Suburban, he waved before pulling onto the street.

"Something new every time I see her," Beth muttered on her way back inside. Hanging up her coat, she faced her mother. "Do you need me to pack for you?"

"Oh, I don't think I'll be going. You'll be busy all day, and I doubt any of my friends will be there."

"There will be plenty of people you know, Mom. If you're up to it, you can help take food outside to the tents."

A surprised smile blossomed on her mother's face. "You'd really let me help?"

"Of course. Now, let's get you packed. You'll have your own cabin for two nights. More, if you want to stay longer."

Showing more energy than Beth had seen in a long time, Donna Jenner jumped up from her chair and hurried down the hall.

"Do you need my help, Mom?"

"Not needed. It won't take long, then we can leave."

Was Beth imagining it, or did her mother sound younger and more alive? Shrugging off the thought, she poured herself another cup of coffee, contenting herself with a cookie as her mother packed.

Jake took a break from supervising the placement of tables inside the tents. The men knew what they were doing. They would do fine without him while he checked on Cisco and talked to Beth.

The gelding had improved a great deal in the last forty-eight hours. The swelling was gone, and he couldn't detect a limp. He'd give Cisco another two days before saddling him for a ride.

Leaving the barn, he stopped to check the sky. Though not the regular rain clouds he'd expect, dark clouds crept in from the north. Not yet worried, Jake would keep watch on the sky. Weather could change within minutes in many of the northern states.

Paying little attention to the people moving about the open area, he stopped at the sound of a car engine a few feet away. Stopping, his gaze swept past the passenger to the driver. Beth met his gaze through the windshield, not hiding her smile or the pleasure she felt at seeing him.

Another look at the passenger confirmed the woman must be her mother. Hurrying to her side of the car, he opened the door.

"Hello, Mrs. Jenner. I'm Jake Kelman." Holding out a hand, he helped her out.

"It's nice to meet you, Mr. Kelman."

"Jake is fine. Is this your bag in the back seat?"

Smiling, she nodded.

"I'll get it. I understand you're staying in the cabin next to Beth. It's real nice."

"Hi, Jake."

"Beth."

Clearing her throat, Donna walked ahead of them. "Where will I find this wonderful cabin?"

"Oh...right. I'll show you," Beth answered.

Gripping the bag tighter, he grinned at Beth. "I'll follow you two."

They'd gone about ten feet when an odd noise came from the direction of the corral beyond the barn. Beth shifted toward him, her eyes wide.

"What was that, Jake?"

"An animal. Let's get your mother to her cabin and I'll check it out."

Beth shook her head. "Give me her bag. You grab a few more men before figuring out what it is." She seemed to realize the order she'd voiced and stilled, her lips drawing into a thin line.

"Anything else, boss?"

"Uh, no. We'll get going." Beth began to turn away, then stopped. "Be careful."

Giving a mock salute, he grinned. "Yes, ma'am."

He waited until the women had made it to Donna's cabin before jogging toward the noise. When it came again, he stopped, pinpointing the location.

"Did you hear that, Jake?"

He didn't look at Brady, keeping his attention on the bushes about thirty yards away. "Yeah. I'm about ready to find out what it is."

Brady whirled around, waving at Jimmy. When he joined Brady and Jake, the noise came again.

"What is that?" Jimmy's hand went to where his ranch gun would normally be around his waist. He'd left it in the bunkhouse.

"Don't know, but I'm going to find out."

"Not alone you aren't. Let me get rifles and we'll all go." Brady didn't wait for an answer before running to the bunkhouse. Less than two minutes later, he returned with three rifles and ammunition.

The three men stuffed the ammunition into their pockets after loading the rifles. Jake studied the area ahead of them, hearing another, weaker growl.

"We'll all go in together. I don't want anyone to approach whatever's out there by themselves. Understood?"

Both men nodded.

"Good. Let's get going."

"Hey, Jake. Wait up." Behind them, Barrel jogged to meet them. "Where you going?"

"There's an animal up in the brush," Jake said. "Probably injured."

"I'll go with you."

"We're good. I'd appreciate it if you'd let Virgil know. We shouldn't be gone more than thirty minutes."

Barrel's brows scrunched together. "If you're certain."

"If we aren't back in an hour, send men to find us."

"Will do, boss." Barrel stood in place as the men approached the hill filled with thick brush and rocks. As he recalled, it was close to where the injured ranch dog, Trooper, had hidden after an animal attack.

Turning on his heels, he hurried to where he'd last seen Virgil. Explaining where Jake had gone, the foreman didn't seem too worried.

"Jake knows what he's doing. Let me know if they don't return within the hour."

Barrel nodded, though he couldn't still his concern for the men. During normal times, checking on what he assumed to be an injured animal wouldn't be cause for worry. These weren't normal days. The wandering rabid pack of wild dogs made all their activities more risky.

The growl came again, though much weaker than before. They'd identified the location as a thick group of bushes to the side of a large boulder.

"What do you want to do, Jake?" Brady shivered as an unexpected icy blast of air whipped around them.

"We stay together. There's the possibility whatever is hiding comes from the rabid pack. Or that the animal isn't alone. We'll take it slow. Stay no more than ten feet apart. Expect to see signs of rabies. And keep your rifles ready." Jake edged closer, his gaze never leaving the bushes ahead of them. "You boys ready?"

"Let's get this over with." Jimmy's voice held a trace of frustration mixed with apprehension.

As they moved forward, a low growl turned to whimpers. Jake heard no other sounds, such as the rustling of other animals, which could signal the pack of dogs.

Spotting movement through the brush ahead, Jake knelt down, his rifle up and ready. What he saw surprised him.

A dog cowered on the snow covered ground, shivering, its wide eyes filled with fear. What he believed to be tan fur was dark gray, as if the dog had rolled in a combination of dirt and oil.

What drew his attention was the dirty collar around the dog's neck. Inching closer, he reached out a gloved hand to the engraved metal name tag. *Duke.*

Jake felt Jimmy and Brady come up beside him. Neither spoke as they watched Jake read the tag.

"Do you think the dog is part of the pack, boss?" Jimmy asked.

"Doesn't seem to be. I think he got separated from his owner and wandered onto the ranch. There isn't blood, but he's hurt somewhere."

Jake let the dog smell his glove. "Hey, Duke. You're a good boy. Are you hurt, buddy?"

The dog whimpered again, trying to crawl closer to Jake. When less than six inches away, intense barking from several dogs reached them, causing Duke to cower back.

"The wild pack is close. We need to get Duke out of here." Jake removed his coat, placing it over the dog while Brady and Jimmy aimed their rifles in the direction of the barking.

Speaking soothing words, Jake lifted Duke, careful to keep the dog's head away from him. Walking back the way they came, his pulse picked up as the sound of the pack got closer.

"They're coming straight toward us." Jimmy picked up his pace to keep up with Jake.

Brady did the same, keeping the rifle firm against his shoulder. Breaking into the open space, he let out a breath at the sight of his cousin, Virgil, and several other ranch hands coming toward them. All carried rifles.

"The wild pack is on the other side of the hill," Jake shouted at the group as he passed by them. "This dog isn't part of the pack."

A few paces later, rifle shots split the air behind him.

Chapter Thirteen

Blasts from the rifles brought other ranch hands running toward the source of the noise. Margie and Anson left their offices in the lodge, while Beth and Abigail stopped what they were doing to step outside. Even Beth's mother, Donna, left her cabin to stand on the front porch. She called to one of the ranch hands as they ran past.

"What's going on?"

"I don't know yet, ma'am."

She made the decision to find out for herself. Grabbing her heavy coat from inside the cabin, she followed others seeking the source of the noise. She came to a stop not far from the back side of the barn.

Jake Kelman knelt on the ground over what appeared to be an injured dog. Several others stood with rifles still in their hands, staring up the hill at another animal sprawled on the ground. Virgil kept his distance while studying the animal.

"I wondered what was going on." Beth stopped next to her mother. "One or both may be part of the wild dog pack which has been roaming near the ranch."

"Wild dogs? Aren't they dangerous?"

"Apparently this pack is more of a threat. Some members are infected with rabies. Game and fish has already searched the area, but weren't able to locate them."

Crossing her arms, Donna nodded toward the hill. "Guess they don't have to search, as the pack is right here."

"They were. Who knows where they're off to now." Beth's attention fixed on Jake, who'd been given a rag to clean the dog in front of him. "I'll be back in a bit, Mom. I'm going to see if Jake has more information."

"I'll come with you."

"It would be better if you stayed here until I talk to Jake."

Dropping her arms, Donna let out a deep sigh. "I'm going back to the cabin. We can talk later about what happened."

Taking a long look at her mother, Beth noticed the deep lines of fatigue on her face, eyes not as bright as usual. "It would be best to rest for a bit. Today is going to be busy."

"Let me know if you need help. I'm happy to pitch in." Donna began the trek to her cabin.

"I'll check on you in a bit, Mom."

Beth made her way to Jake, glancing down at the dog, who stood beside him. "Is this one part of the pack?"

"I don't think so. My guess is he got separated from his home and the pack went after him. He's got a collar and name tag. Duke." Jake ran a hand down the dog's back.

"The closest neighbors are at least a mile away. Whoever his owners are, he's a long way from home. I hope he wasn't dropped off and forgotten." She dropped down beside Jake, her gaze landing on soft brown, inquisitive eyes. "Will he let me pet him?"

"He's had no problem with me. Run your hand down his back."

She did, getting nuzzled in return. "He's such a sweetheart. Once he's cleaned up, Duke will be a beauty."

"I'm going to talk with Doc Worrel. Maybe someone's notified her of a lost dog."

Beth pursed her lips in thought. "Lydia, who owns Brilliance Coffee & Bakery, has a bulletin board in the front. People post notices of lost pets on it. There must be other businesses who allow posting of lost and found pets. Do you know anything about the animal that was shot?"

Jake glanced toward where Virgil and Wyatt stood by the downed dog. "I'm sure it was part of the pack that was chasing Duke."

"With the wild dogs so close, I wonder if Margie should consider cancelling Thanksgiving dinner."

"No, I won't be cancelling anything." Neither had noticed Margie walking up behind them. "I spoke with Anson, Wyatt, and Virgil. They're going to assign men to watch for the dogs. Anson called the local warden, who always brings his family to the ranch for Thanksgiving. He agrees the pack is unlikely to attack with the large number of people who'll be here. And who do we have here?"

Jake pointed to the tag. "This is Duke. I believe he's the reason the pack is so close."

"You mean, they were chasing him?" She reached out, touching Duke's fur.

"That's my guess. Beth and I have been discussing ways to locate his owner." Shoving himself up, Jake did his best to brush off the snow. Beth did the same.

"Besides the obvious, we could make up flyers and post them around," Margie said. "I'm going back to the house. See you two later."

"I'd better get back to the kitchen. Most everything is ready. Still, there's always more to do." Beth placed a hand on Jake's arm. "Let me know how I can help you with Duke."

Smiling, an unfamiliar warmth crept through him at her touch. "Thanks, Beth. I'll see you soon."

Tilting her head to one side, she raised a brow.

Chuckling, he lowered his hand to pet Duke. "The men and I will be there to take the food out to the tents."

She felt her face heat. "Oh, yes. Of course. Abigail and I will be ready for you."

Beth released a deep sigh of relief. Most of the food had been delivered to the serving tables, the guests were laughing and smiling as they ate, and there'd been no further sightings of the wild dogs.

"Let's put the rest of the desserts on plates to take outside," Beth said. "Are all the pumpkin pies gone?"

Abigail checked the pie storage chest. "There are three left. Do you want me to slice them?"

"Keep one for Margie and Anson, and plate the rest. Pumpkin is their favorite."

A deafening boom caught them off guard, shaking the doors and windows. "What was that?"

Beth dashed to the window. The sky had darkened over the last few hours. "It hasn't started snowing, but it won't be long." She turned to face Abigail. "This isn't good."

Jake walked in with Brady and Barrel. "The guests are getting a little restless. The wind has picked up considerably. There appears to be a major snowstorm coming from the north. I give it less than thirty minutes before it hits us."

Beth checked the time. Three-thirty. "It's early to close everything up."

"It's doubtful anyone else will arrive with the approaching storm," Abigail said. "What do you think, Jake?"

"I agree with you. My suggestion is we assist any guests who need help to their cars, bring the food inside, and lower the tents. I can get several more men to help out. It's your decision, Beth."

The windows and doors shook again as another large gust of wind slammed against the lodge. "Better get started right away."

"I'll help them." Abigail grabbed her coat and followed them outside.

Beth joined them after clearing the large counter for the food from outside. Entering the first tent, she saw most of the visitors had already left. Savvy with the way the weather could move from beautiful to nasty in little time, they'd loaded their vehicles and driven off without having to be persuaded.

"How can we help?" Margie noticed the progress they'd already made in the first tent, not waiting for a response. "Let's grab the tablecloths first, Donna. Daisy and Lily are already in the second tent, Beth."

"Wonderful. We'll join them once we're finished here. Jake wants to tear down the tents before the storm worsens."

"I'll let Wyatt know. I'm sure he'll want to help."

"That's great, Margie." Beth stilled at the sudden gust shaking all sides of the tent.

"Let's get the rest of the tables out of here, boys." Jake tried to shout above the noise from the wind.

Several ranch hands joined them, carrying the tables outside to stack under the eaves of the lodge. With luck, they wouldn't be covered in snow before the rental company returned on Friday.

The first tent had been torn down when a car he didn't recognize parked by the barn. An older model with light pink paint and a ragtop, Jake watched as a tall figure emerged from the passenger seat.

His chest tightened. "It can't be." Bundled up in a heavy coat with hood made it hard for him to be sure. Then the person turned to face him, and his good mood evaporated. *Helena.*

"Jake! Hey. It's me." Waving her hand in the air, she hurried toward him. The unmistakable frown on his face slowed her progress. Stopping a few feet away, she bit her lower lip, trying to regain a smile. "Aren't you glad to see me?"

"I'm glad you're safe, Helena. But no, I'm not pleased you drove all the way south."

"I thought you'd be pleased."

"You knew that wouldn't be true. It's the type of stunt you always pull. I'll see if there's a place you can sleep for the night. Tomorrow, you should plan to drive home."

"Hey, Jake. We're tearing down the second tent." Jimmy jogged toward them, stopping when he didn't recognize the woman. "Do you have time to help?"

"On my way. Look, Helena, I don't have time to visit with you. With the storm almost on us, you shouldn't be driving. Follow me." Opening the door to the lodge, he indicated several large, upholstered chairs. "Stay in here until I can figure things out. There's a bathroom through those doors."

"Maybe I can help."

He winced at the pouty tone of her voice. "Not now. Just do me a favor and stay here. And please don't wander around. I'll show you the place when I'm done."

"But..."

Rubbing the back of his neck, he took what he hoped would be a calming breath. "Helena. Please. Just stay in here. I'll be back as soon as I can."

Walking to the window, she watched him dash toward a large tent where a group of people worked. Feeling shunted aside, Helena turned to face the large great room of the lodge.

She muttered incoherent thoughts to herself while walking around the huge space. Angry at Jake's lack of enthusiasm, she poked her head into the large kitchen. The center work island was covered in food.

"Probably from outside," she said aloud, not caring if anyone heard her. Picking up a slice of cold turkey, she hurried to eat it, surprised at the hunger it triggered. Several slices of turkey and ham later, she spotted a plate of brownies. Unable to stop herself, she ate three before her stomach rebelled.

Locating a glass, she filled it with water, watching out the window as the snow increased. Still curious, Helena opened and closed cupboards until coming across a refrigerator filled with wine.

Desire for a glass of red wine almost took control before she closed the door. Jake's anger would triple if he came back to find her drinking wine. It wasn't the way she wanted to start her campaign to win him back.

A campaign she couldn't afford to lose.

Chapter Fourteen

It took longer than anticipated to tear down and store the second tent. Every time Jake glanced at Beth, he found her watching him before lowering her gaze.

He'd hoped they would've had time to talk after everyone was sated from her excellent food. Instead, the storm moved in, squelching his plans.

And now he had to contend with Helena. Jake thought he'd been clear about finding friends near her home to share Thanksgiving. Then again, she'd always interpreted everything in her own, self-centered way, disregarding anyone's wishes except her own.

Finished outside, he spotted Beth and Abigail heading back into the lodge. His sister knew Helena. Though they'd never been best friends, Abigail knew of Helena's struggle with alcohol. What would she say when spotting his old girlfriend in the lodge?

Putting her up for the night would mean someone had to clean one of the vacant cabins. There was no doubt in his mind that someone would be him.

Shivering as a gust of snow slammed against him, he entered the lodge. The door to the kitchen stood open, soft voices wafted out into the dining room. He recognized Abigail's voice, then Helena's. A good sign.

Slowing his steps as he approached the kitchen, he cleared his throat. "I see you stayed right where I asked you to."

"I was bored, Jake. You couldn't have thought I'd just sit there until you returned."

"That's exactly what I expected, Helena."

Abigail stood between the two, biting her lower lip. She understood Jake's concern. Helena had a long history of pilfering items she could sell for alcohol. Glancing around, she saw nothing missing. Looking at Helena's tight jeans and sweater, it would be hard to conceal anything.

"I'm hungry. Is it all right if I eat some of the food on the counter?"

Abigail nodded. "Of course, Helena. I'll prepare a plate for you."

"Then we need to figure out what to do with you." The edge in Jake's voice wasn't missed on either woman.

Crossing her arms, Helena leaned against a counter. "You're making me feel bad for coming. I thought you'd be thrilled to see me."

Pinching the bridge of his nose, he shook his head. "I was clear you weren't to come to Whistle Rock Ranch. The timing couldn't be worse."

"Well, I wanted to see you." Taking the plate Abigail prepared, she picked up a slice of ham with her fingers. "Hmmm. This is delicious." She picked up a fork and knife, scooping up red potatoes. "Everything is so good, Abbie. Are you the cook?"

"Assistant."

"Sounds great. Maybe I can find a job like yours. By the way, where should I put my things?"

Abigail looked at her brother and shrugged.

Jake's jaw clenched as he worked to control his frustration. "If the storm clears, you'll be driving home tonight."

"But…"

Holding up his hand, he stopped whatever Helena meant to say. "If the storm continues, we'll find an extra bed for the night and you can drive back after breakfast. Those are your only two choices."

"What if I want to stay?"

"Do you have enough money for an apartment, food, and gas while you look for a job?"

"You know I don't, Jake."

"Then it's best for you to go home." He took a step closer to her, setting a hand on her shoulder. "I'm not saying this to be mean. You need to make your own way, and not always rely on me to get out of trouble. I'm not that person any longer, Helena."

Her lower lip jutted out in her patented pout. "Do you have a girlfriend?"

"Not your business."

The lip jutted out even further. He ignored it.

"I have work to do. Abigail, can Helena hang with you for a while? Better yet, she can help you and Beth clean up the kitchen."

"Oh, that would be great. Helena, there are aprons hanging on the wall over there." Pointing across the room,

Abigail sent a conspiratorial glance at Jake. "We'll be done in no time at all."

"I guess I can help you." Walking as if she'd been sentenced to life in prison, she lifted an apron from a hook. "Who's Beth?"

"She's the chef. I'm her assistant."

Tying the apron around her waist, she looked around. "Shouldn't she be here working with us?"

"In most restaurants, the chef doesn't do any clean-up. Beth does help, so we're lucky. She'll be here sometime." Lips twitching at the corners, Abigail looked away.

"All right. I'm going to check out where Helena can bunk down tonight."

"We should still be here. After cleaning up, we'll be setting up food for dinner."

The groan Helena couldn't stop was ignored.

"You ladies enjoy yourselves." He mouthed a *thank you* to Abigail, knowing he'd owe her big time.

Beth didn't move from her spot in the hall behind the kitchen. She hadn't meant to eavesdrop. It just sort of happened.

From the conversation, it was clear the woman named Helena had gone against Jake's wishes and crashed the Bonner party. It was also clear the two had a history...a long one, if Beth were to guess.

She'd poked her head around the corner long enough to see a tall, lithe, beautiful woman who could be a model for skinny jeans. And form-fitting sweaters made of cotton with enough spandex to catch a man's attention. Somehow, Jake had seemed oblivious to Helena's beauty or figure.

The entire conversation had left a bitter taste in her mouth. Beth had been toying with the idea of inviting Jake to share dessert and coffee with her after the dinner service. It had taken her all day to work up the courage to ask him. She knew her idea would have to wait.

Her feelings for the tall, lanky cowboy had slapped her in the face during their walk. Beth had been attracted to him since they'd met a few months earlier. Focusing on her work, staying long hours in the kitchen, then retiring to her cabin, she'd staved off any chance her feelings would grow beyond friendship.

Then he'd invited her on *the* walk. Beth had begun thinking of their short stroll around the ranch that way. Jake had held out his hand, and she'd accepted it. So easy and so hard.

Unexpected, the invitation had come when she'd most desired companionship. Solitude became old after a while.

The walk had been perfect and much too brief.

Shaking off thoughts of the previous night, she joined Abigail and Helena in the kitchen. Even with a huge Thanksgiving meal, the men would still expect dinner. At the minimum, sliced ham, turkey, and other leftovers.

"Hello, Beth. This is an old friend of mine," Abigail said.

"And Jake's," Helena added.

"Yes, and Jake's. Beth, this is Helena. Helena, Beth. She's the magic behind all the wonderful meals we prepare at Whistle Rock."

"Nice to meet you, Helena." Noticing the apron the woman wore, Beth grinned. She'd heard Jake's suggestion she help Abigail clean up the considerable mess on the large counter. "It appears you're all set to help us pack up leftovers and wash dishes."

Helena glanced away. "It wasn't really my idea."

Beth ignored the comment. "Even so, we appreciate your help." She tapped a finger against her lips as if thinking. "Abigail and I will put the food away while you begin rinsing and loading the dishwashers." She nodded at the two commercial units to the side of the large sink.

"I'd rather pack."

"It will all move faster with us packing the food, Helena. Rinsing is very easy, as the dishwashers are industrial quality."

Helena pursed her lips. "What does that mean?"

"They're strong enough to clean food off the serving plates, bowls, and utensils. Since we used paper and plastic, there isn't a great deal of work. Abigail, please grab the containers we use for leftovers."

"Will do."

"When we're finished, we'll decide what to set out for dinner."

"I'm pretty sure the men will eat whatever we warm up for them." Abigail set a handful of containers on the counter. "I'll get more if needed."

Beth sent careful glances at Helena. She'd never seen anyone work at such a slow pace. Deciding the best way to deal with Helena was to ignore her, she concentrated on packing food. As she worked, Beth set aside meat, chicken, and vegetables, which would be easy to reheat.

"Are there leftover rolls, Abigail?"

"About three dozen that haven't been baked. There are also maybe two dozen that could be reheated."

"Perfect. We can set out condiments for those who'd prefer to fix sandwiches."

"Jake doesn't like sandwiches."

Beth and Abigail looked up from what they were doing to stare at Helena.

"That's not true," Abigail said. "I've seen him eat sandwiches plenty of times."

Helena turned toward them, placing a hand on one hip. "He never ate them around me."

Beth could see where this was going, deciding to intervene. "Doesn't matter. He can choose, the same as everyone else."

The three continued in silence until the door opened and Margie entered. "You ladies need any help?"

"Thanks, but we have this," Beth said.

Margie looked over her shoulder. "Anything left for the food bank?"

"We saved two full turkeys and one ham. Both need to be carved and packaged."

"Great, Beth. Assuming the weather clears, I'll drive into town tomorrow."

Helena whirled around. "May I go with you?"

Without answering, Margie walked toward her, stopping a foot away. "I don't believe we've met. I'm Margie Bonner."

Her eyes widened, recognizing the last name. "Nice to meet you. I'm Helena Thomas."

"I don't recognize the name. Are you from Brilliance?"

"Uh, no, ma'am. I'm from up north."

"Wyoming or Montana?"

"Wyoming, ma'am. I'm a friend of Abigail and Jake."

Brows arched, Margie's gaze narrowed on her. "I see. I'll be leaving about eight in the morning. You're welcome to ride along. In fact, you can help deliver the packages to the local community cupboard."

"Is the bus station close?"

"I'll take you there after we're finished. As I recall, there's a bus going north around eleven."

"That would be perfect, Mrs. Bonner. Thank you."

Margie didn't correct her. Few people around Brilliance called her Mrs. Bonner. Something about Helena troubled her. Deciding she was being too critical, she headed out the back door.

"I'll be here to load the truck at seven. That will give us plenty of time to get to town." She directed the comment to everyone, though her gaze landed on Helena.

"Yes, ma'am."

The door closing echoed off the hard surfaces of the kitchen. Beth had picked up on Margie's hesitancy regarding Helena, doubting either of the younger women had noticed. She had to agree with her boss's instincts. Something she couldn't quite identify also bothered Beth about Helena. Knowing the woman would be gone tomorrow morning, Beth let the thought slide from her mind.

Chapter Fifteen

Jake idled the truck, waiting as the ranch hands dumped the last of the hay onto the ground. Much of the previous snow had melted off, allowing the cattle to graze. Yesterday's storm covered the ground in several inches of snow, requiring the delivery of food to the herd.

He'd said his goodbyes to Helena, even loaded much of the food, before she and Margie drove to town. An odd, unsettled feeling had landed in the pit of his stomach when she waved through the window.

"That was much too easy," he muttered to himself as he climbed into the truck. Two hours later, the unease hadn't left him.

Parking the truck in its spot near the barn, Jake heeded the urge to speak with Beth. She and Abigail worked together at the large counter, assembling what appeared to be skewers of beef and chicken with vegetables. He ignored the way his stomach growled at the thought of lunch.

Beth greeted him first. "Hey, Jake. Can we get you something?"

"Whatever you're making there would be great." He sauntered to the coffee pot, pouring a full cup. Blowing across the top, he took a sip. "Everything work out all right with Helena?"

Abigail stopped what she was doing, saying nothing for a long moment. "Something's off with her. Not sure what, other than I know she's fighting her urge for alcohol."

"How do you know she's fighting it and not giving in?" Jake set the cup down next to the sink.

"I saw her pull out a bottle of wine, stare at it for a long time before returning it to its spot. Later, she did the same with a bottle of Anson's whiskey. He really should keep his liquor locked away somewhere." Abigail lowered her head, continuing to prepare skewers.

"I've told Anson the same," Beth said. "Do you have a bad feeling about Helena being here, Jake?"

"Not really. Well...maybe." Picking up the cup, he drained the contents, placing it in the sink. "The same as Abigail, something's not right about her visit. She gave up too easily about not staying. My experience with her is she claws at something until you give in and let her have what she wants. Getting her to leave the ranch was much too easy."

"She jumped right onto Margie's comment about driving to town." Abigail set down the last skewer. "And she never mentioned talking to you, Jake."

Beth nodded in agreement. "Margie's reaction to her wasn't as warm as usual."

He pinned her with a pointed stare. "What do you mean?"

Shrugging, Beth set down her knife. "I've never seen Margie be anything but welcoming to people she meets. She was guarded with Helena, even a little cool. I believe she might have been happy to get her off the ranch.”

Jake rubbed the back of his neck, lips twisting in a grimace. “That *is* odd.” Debating whether or not to pour a second cup of coffee, he decided against it. “I’d better get back out with the men.”

“Do you have time to talk for a minute, Jake?”

“I do, Beth.”

“Pour the second cup of coffee you know you want. We can talk in the dining room.”

Chuckling, he refilled the cup, following her through the swinging doors. Beth had already taken a seat at a table away from the others. Sitting next to her, he set the cup down.

“What is it you want to talk about?”

Shifting in her chair, Beth suddenly believed this was a bad idea. A very bad idea. It meant giving Jake a peek into her deepest feelings. Unless…

Setting her cup of tea on the table, she rested both hands in her lap. “I’m going to be making some different desserts on Saturday. I thought you might want to test them with me.”

Leaning back in his chair, Jake’s grin spread across his face. “Just me and you?”

“Yes. Just the two of us. Are you interested?”

“Absolutely. How about I take you to town for dinner on Saturday, then we come here to test desserts?”

“You want to take me to dinner?”

“Well, yes. If you’re interested.”

"What about dinner for everyone else?"

"Is Abigail able to handle serving the employees?"

"Well, yes. I mean, if she agrees."

A slow grin from Jake was her answer. They both knew Abigail would agree.

"So, is that a yes? I take you to dinner and you supply the dessert?"

Before Beth could answer, the door to Anson's office flew open. The red faced patriarch of Whistle Rock Ranch stormed to his wife's office, shoving the door open. Finding his wife gone, he spotted them at the table.

"Someone was in my office." He glared at the duo, more in shock than in an accusatory manner. "They took close to five thousand dollars from my desk drawer. Either of you seen someone snooping around?"

Jake's gaze locked with Beth's, both afraid they had a good idea who might've taken Anson's money.

After a minimal explanation, Jake and Beth climbed into his truck, heading to the Brilliance bus stop. Anson was right behind them in his truck.

A quick phone call to Margie confirmed she'd dropped Helena off at the bus station an hour earlier. If they hurried, there was a chance they'd be able to arrive before the bus began its journey north.

The roads didn't cooperate. Icy from the storm the day before, both drivers were forced to travel below the speed limit by a good fifteen miles per hour.

"If the bus leaves, I'll follow it until she gets off." Jake couldn't recall a time he'd been so angry. "I never should've allowed her to stay."

"There wasn't much you could do."

"I could've put her right back on a bus north."

Reaching across the center console, she squeezed his arm. "We don't know for sure it was Helena who took the money."

Glancing at her hand, his voice softened. "Who else would've dared steal from Anson?"

She didn't answer. Didn't have to. Both knew Helena was the only person unfamiliar with those who lived at Whistle Rock.

"I left her alone in the lodge. Found her in the kitchen. She had plenty of time to go through the offices and find Anson's money. It's my fault his money is missing."

"That is not true, Jake. If Helena did steal it, she's the one to blame." She squeezed his arm again before drawing her hand away.

Pulling into a parking space close to the bus station, he jumped out, rushing to the office. He knew the efforts were wasted. The bus had already left.

Meeting Anson outside, he apologized for his lack of judgment.

"Not your fault, Jake." Pulling his phone from a pocket, Anson called the sheriff. After relaying the basic of what happened, he looked back at Jake. "What's her name?"

"Helena Thomas."

Anson relayed the information, hanging up soon afterward. "The bus will be stopped and Helena questioned. If she took the money, they'll take her into custody."

"If I left now, I could intercept the bus."

"Appreciate the offer, Jake. Let's rely on the law to take care of this. I was a fool not to lock the drawer and my office with so many people at the ranch on Thanksgiving. Never had a problem before." Placing a hand on Jake's shoulder, he turned them toward their trucks. "We'll head home and wait to hear from the sheriff."

The truck's cab stayed eerily silent as Jake drove back to the ranch. Despite Anson's words, he knew the responsibility for the theft landed on him. He didn't need Anson or Beth to tell him Helena's sticky hands weren't the ones to steal the money. In his heart, Jake knew she was the thief.

Parking the truck, they looked at each other, Beth the first to speak. "I have to get ready for lunch. Do you still want to take me to dinner tomorrow night?"

He didn't have to force a smile. "Nothing's changed. I'll come by your cabin at six."

"Come by the kitchen. I want to do what I can for Abigail before we leave. Please let me know what happens with Helena."

"I'm sure Anson will get back to me soon." Unable to shake his disappointment, with a slight wave, Jake headed toward the barn.

When Jake hadn't heard from Anson by dinner, he found him in Margie's office. Anson, Margie, Wyatt, and Daisy stopped their conversation at his knock.

"Sorry to interrupt. Did you hear back from the sheriff?"

Anson gave a brisk nod. "Sure did. Your Helena was on the bus with my money. The sheriff will bring it by tomorrow."

"What about Helena?"

"She's in custody, waiting for arraignment. He told me if she doesn't have a record, she'll probably get off pretty easy. Hopefully, the experience will scare her enough to never pull this on anyone else."

"I hope you're right, Anson. Again—"

Holding up a hand, Anson shook his head. "Not your fault, Jake. Don't ever think it was."

"All right. Thanks." Closing the office door behind him, his gaze moved to the kitchen.

Everyone had left the dining room, which meant Beth and Abigail were cleaning up after the meal. He hesitated a mere minute before deciding to find her.

They appeared to be finishing up for the evening. "Hey."

The women looked up at his brief greeting, Abigail offering a faint smile compared to Beth's wide, bright one. She finished drying the pot before walking to him.

"Did you find out anything about the money?"

He explained what Anson had learned. "I haven't heard from her and don't expect to."

"Maybe it's for the best. She took advantage of you, Jake. My guess is she's too embarrassed to call." For a second time in hours, Beth placed a hand on his arm.

"She hasn't called because they confiscated her phone." Abigail had stopped putting plates away to look their way. "Helena's always thought she could get away with anything. Maybe she'll get over herself and grow up."

"Aren't you being a little harsh?"

"You haven't known her for long, Beth. Jake and I have seen the damage she can do. It's time something happens to wake her up. If it doesn't, she may end up in jail for a long time."

Jake covered Beth's hand with his. "She's right. Helena's been working toward this for years. I'm certain she's done this before."

"But never got caught," Abigail said.

Beth offered a grave nod. "Yeah. At least Anson found the answer to who took his money."

As the room quieted, Jake's hand threaded with Beth's. "Do you have time for a walk?"

"Go on, Beth. I'll finish in here."

"Thanks, Abigail. See you in the morning."

"Just don't do anything I wouldn't do." Abigail grinned as the red crept up Beth's cheeks.

Chapter Sixteen

Jake took a different route around the ranch from their previous walk. Partly due to the additional snow, but mostly because it would take longer to get Beth to her cabin.

Their entwined fingers felt right. Perfect, in fact, as they walked past the parking area and barn. Jake wished he had something clever to say, a witty comment that would make her smile. Although he'd heard many talented cowboy poets and storytellers at various annual gatherings, he wasn't one of those men. Turned out, he didn't have to worry about it.

"I'm so glad Thanksgiving is over." Beth released a slow, labored breath. "With Nacho gone, I was certain something would happen."

"What happened was everyone loved your food. The day was a success. Except for Helena showing up." Grimacing at his own words, he shook his head. "And that's the last I'm bringing her up. Did you have a chance to talk to your brothers?"

"Not yesterday. I spoke with them today. Something came up…" She hesitated, deciding if she should share more.

He squeezed her hand. "Something came up?"

Just then, her phone rang. Checking caller ID, she shook her head. "Excuse me a minute." Walking a few feet away, she turned her back to him to answer the call. "I don't know who you are, but I've captured your phone number. My next step is to give it to the local authorities. Soon, you'll have to call from a jail cell." Hanging up, she turned back toward him.

"Feel better now?" His grin had her smiling.

"You heard what I said?"

"Couldn't help it. Voices carry in the night air." His features sobered. "Are you being harassed?" Reaching out, he took her hand, drawing her closer.

"It turns out my older brother, Julian, and I are both receiving harassing calls. We've been keeping them to ourselves, not wanting to alarm our mother or anyone else. Now that it's out in the open, we're going to be more proactive in stopping them."

"What does the caller say?"

"First, the voice is electronically modified, so we can't be sure it's a man. The call starts out friendly, as if we're old friends. The following sentences hint at wrongdoing by my family and how the caller will make us pay for what we've done. Nothing too blatant. Nothing that could be taken to the authorities. The perfect method of intimidation without a direct threat."

"What about your other brother? Is he getting the same calls?"

"Thomas had no idea what was going on."

"Who do you think it is?" He guided them toward the corral holding several older mares. Though it was later, a couple fed from the hay spread on the ground.

"That's the thing. Julian believes it could be a disgruntled employee. A male executive they had to fire because of unethical behavior. Julian and his wife both agree he's the type to hold a grudge. If they're right, I have no idea why he would harass me."

"To get to Julian. Your brother can't be happy you're getting the calls."

"No, he isn't. We're going to talk again to tomorrow. Julian is smart. He'll think of something."

"Meaning you'd rather not talk about it anymore tonight?"

"Right."

"Then we won't."

Walking the perimeter of the corral, Jake slowed his steps to take in the gorgeous night. "Traveling with the rodeo, I've visited a lot of places. Not one is as beautiful as a Wyoming night in winter."

"It is wonderful here. I was concerned living on a ranch wouldn't work for me. As the months go by, I become more certain this is exactly where I'm meant to be. Maybe not for life, but for a good while."

Taking in her words, Jake felt his throat and chest tighten. Her plans and his couldn't be more different. She wanted a home, a sense of being settled. More than anything, he wanted one more chance at rodeoing. His career had ended on an injury. Not the way he wanted to go out. With his leg healed, he could now put serious thought into returning for at least one season.

"What about you, Jake? Do you see yourself staying at Whistle Rock for a few years?"

"Guess I haven't been here long enough to decide."

"That sounds as if you might leave much sooner than later."

"It just means I haven't made any decisions."

"Oh." They stood a moment longer, looking toward the Tetons. "It's getting late. Maybe we should start back."

Without answering, he headed toward the cabins. "Someday, I want a ranch of my own."

"You can't get that by working here and saving for it?"

Jake forgot Beth didn't know he'd made good money competing in rodeos. Enough to buy a ranch now, which he planned to do as soon as he'd fulfilled his rodeo dream.

"Maybe."

Stopping, she turned to look up at him. "You do know Wyatt and Virgil are expecting you to stay with the ranch for a while."

"Yeah, I know. I haven't committed to anything."

"I see." Taking the few remaining steps to her cabin, she turned, flashing a smile she didn't feel. "Thank you for the walk. I enjoyed it."

Bending down, he brushed an unexpected kiss across her cheek. "I'm sorry I didn't have the answers you expected."

Still a little stunned from the impromptu kiss, she again looked up at him. "It's your life, Jake. You have to do what's right for your future."

What if I want you in my future? he thought. Instead, he let the question go unasked.

"I don't have to decide for a while. We still have time for many more evening walks. Right, Beth?"

A slow grin tipped the corners of her mouth. "Anytime you want."

Beth woke to her phone ringing. Believing it was her mother, she answered. "Hello, Mom." The response was the familiar silence, then the electronic voice. The message hadn't changed. Instead of feeling vulnerable, she became angry.

"I have nothing to do with your being fired. My recommendation is to find another job and stop harassing me and my brother."

Instead of her hanging up, the caller did it for her. Beth hoped mentioning details might stop the calls.

Taking a quick shower, she dressed, thinking of the call. She wondered if informing the sheriff might help. She'd met Garth Duggan at the Thanksgiving dinner. Not much older than her, she recalled someone mentioned him being a single father and just winning a second four-year term as the county sheriff. Maybe she'd drive to town the first of the week to talk with him.

Leaving her cabin, she glanced at Jake's cabin, seeing a light on. Their discussion the night before had kept her awake as she let his words roll around in her head.

She'd believed he'd stay for at least a full dude ranch season. Which meant until October of next year. The thought he'd leave early tasted as bitter as the pills the doctor gave her as a child.

Noticing a light snow drifting down, she pulled the hood of her coat up and rushed to the kitchen's back door. Stomping her boots on the stoop, she shook the snow from her coat and stepped inside.

At four-thirty in the morning, she didn't expect any activity. Instead, Abigail cooked bacon and sausages while taking occasional sips of coffee. There'd be plenty of time to make pancakes, eggs, and coffee before the men arrived at six.

"Good morning." Sliding off her coat, Beth placed it on a hook, then exchanged boots for thick-soled work shoes. "How long have you been up?"

Setting her coffee down, she didn't look up from frying the meat. "I woke up at three and couldn't get back to sleep. Bacon and sausage are easy to make ahead and keep warm."

Beth took a moment to study Abigail. She'd seen her smile maybe twice since coming to the ranch. It was obvious something weighed on her, yet Beth didn't believe it was her place to ask. It might be best to ask Jake if he knew what worried his sister.

As if she'd conjured him up, Jake walked in the back door. "Is there coffee available?"

"Enough for a few cups," Abigail answered. "If you're taking it with you, I'll get a to-go mug."

"Two of them would be great. Virgil's going with me." Focusing on Beth for the first time, his features relaxed. "Good morning."

"Good morning. If you're heading out, I can wrap up some bacon and sausages."

"Appreciate it. Virgil got a call from the game warden. A neighbor to the south reported several of his cattle being slaughtered. Probably by wolves. Wyatt wants us to check it out."

"Could it be the wild dogs?" Beth placed enough food for two in a large plastic bag, handing it to him.

"Might be. Our cattle have already been moved closer, and the horses are safe. We're heading over to take a look around and find out if the neighbor needs any help."

"Be careful."

"Thanks, Beth. I intend to." Sending a meaningful look at his sister, he stepped into the growing storm.

Jake's thoughts were on Beth as Virgil drove toward their neighbor's ranch. They'd meet at the house and go from there.

"What's his place like?" Jake bit into another piece of bacon, offering the bag to Virgil.

"About half the size of Whistle Rock. It was started by his great-grandfather, and from what Anson says, it's profitable. He raises premium beef and pork, selling the meat to high-end restaurants and specialty stores around the northwest. His son is in charge of marketing. Word is, the son has no desire to take over the place when his father retires."

"He could hire a strong foreman and continue his marketing activities."

"He could," Virgil said. "That's just what I've heard. His dad is in his seventies. Mother died a few years ago."

"Then whatever happens might be soon."

"Might be." Keeping his focus on the road, Virgil reached into the bag, removed a sausage link.

The men fell into a comfortable silence during the last mile. The storm had increased. If it continued, they could find another foot of snow on the ground by mid-afternoon.

But Jake's thoughts weren't on the snow or the slaughtered cattle. They were on what might happen to the ranch if the current owner decided to sell.

Chapter Seventeen

The damage turned out to be somewhat less than Jake anticipated. One animal had been attacked. While he spoke to the rancher, Seth Magnus, Virgil studied the tracks.

"I don't think it was wolves." Virgil moved his fingers over indentations in the snow. "The tracks are closer to those of the wild dog pack that's plagued our ranch."

"Heard about that," Magnus said. "Until now, they haven't attacked my cattle."

"You've been lucky," Virgil said. "I'd suggest getting the warden out here to take a look. It's a rabid pack. Real dangerous to animals and people."

Magnus's face, chiseled from years of sun and wind, didn't change with Virgil's words. Not even a nod of understanding. Instead, he whirled around, climbed into his truck, and drove away.

"Guess Magnus doesn't have a mobile phone. Any reason we need to stick around?"

Virgil shook his head. "No." Pulling out his phone as he walked to the truck, he called the warden. After reporting the attack, he slid the phone back into his pocket. "In case Magnus doesn't report it."

Climbing into the truck, Jake clicked the seat belt into place. "Wish there was something we could do about the wild pack. They attack, then become ghosts. Few tracks to follow. It's too dangerous to post men beyond the safety of the lodge and bunkhouse."

"It's been a long time since we've faced this type of problem. I believe Wyatt and I were boys. We should talk to Anson about what's been done in the past."

Jake nodded in agreement, his thoughts already shifting to Seth Magnus and the possibility he might sell his ranch. It would be tricky to approach the grizzled rancher directly. He'd have to think about how he saw his future.

Should he stay at Whistle Rock Ranch for a few years? Try again for another season with the rodeo? Allow his feelings for Beth to grow? None of the questions rolling around in his head were easy to answer.

Beth hunched over the desk in one corner of the kitchen, sketching out a menu for Margie. She'd decided to hold a dinner party before Christmas. Not some small, intimate affair for ten.

Invitations for thirty people would be sent the following day for a semi-formal dinner on a Saturday evening. Margie requested a creative menu, similar to what Beth would've served during the holidays at the resort in Jackson.

She stared at her list, scratching off some items while adding others. Margie expected to have three options by the end of the day. Thank goodness she had this quiet time for a couple hours after lunch.

It had been a few days since she'd spoken with Jake. Beth didn't want to believe he was avoiding her, just too busy to come into the kitchen.

She'd heard about the attack on cattle at a neighboring ranch. Everyone on Whistle Rock Ranch walked around on edge, wondering when the next attack would occur. Or if the dogs would begin stalking people.

At least her own, human stalker hadn't called since her last warning about contacting the sheriff. The calls to her brother had also stopped. Perhaps their harasser had given up.

Beth jolted when her phone rang. Checking the caller's identity, she sighed, knowing she should've blocked his number.

It had been months since she'd heard from him. Not long enough in her opinion.

"Hello."

"Beth. It's Freddie. How are you?"

"Great. Why are you calling?"

His voice sounded distant, as if he were in a tunnel. "What if I just wanted to hear your voice?"

"I'd assume you weren't being truthful. Where are you?"

"New York City, at a convention. I remembered us being here together last year and decided to call."

"Enjoy your mental stroll down memory lane. I'm too busy for that. Bye."

"Wait!"

"Is there something you want?" The pause extended long enough she thought Freddie wouldn't respond.

"I get back to Jackson in a few days and thought I'd drive to Brilliance. We could have dinner somewhere."

"No thanks. Anything else?"

"Come on, Beth. All I want is to see you."

"In case you've forgotten, you have a girlfriend."

"All I'm asking for is dinner. Besides, the girlfriend moved away a couple weeks ago."

"Sorry to hear it. I'm still not interested in seeing you. We aren't going to be best buddies, Freddie. Look, I'm in the middle of a special project for my boss and need to go. Have a safe flight home." She hung up before he could plead his case again.

After getting to know a little bit about Jake, Beth didn't know what she ever saw in Freddie.

They'd had to postpone their dinner in town for a week due to additional work at the ranch. It turned out for the best, as Beth needed time to consider his lack of commitment to Whistle Rock.

She'd already decided to stay at least two years. With her mother in town, the decision wasn't hard.

Looking back down at her menu, she made some final changes before picking up the paper. She'd decided the best way to present her suggestions to Margie would be the same way it had been done at the resort.

Watching for Jake on the way to her cabin, she waved away a stab of disappointment when she didn't spot him.

Maybe he'd stop by after dinner. She'd love another walk. Since he'd been honest about not knowing his future at the ranch, which meant his future with her, Beth had decided to take their friendship a day at a time. She'd enjoy being with him while not reading anything more into their relationship.

Sitting down at the small desk in her cabin, she pulled up a program which made it easy to create a beautiful one page menu. Margie would appreciate the extra step while giving her boss an idea of what would be placed at each place setting.

Reading from her notes, Beth selected a template and began. Her fingers moved easily over the keys, and within minutes, the menu was ready to show Margie. Planning to print it at the lodge, she copied the design to a flash drive.

The weather had changed since entering her cabin. Giant snowflakes stuck to the frozen ground, and the temperature had dropped at least ten degrees.

Closing the zipper on her heavy coat, she dashed across the short distance to the kitchen's back door. Turning back before going inside, her gaze locked on Jake, who stood outside the barn, waving his arms at her. The gesture surprised and excited her.

Jogging toward her, she was the recipient of a broad grin. "Hey." He stopped next to her.

"Hey, yourself." She hoped he couldn't hear her heart thumping. The same reaction occurred often when he was near. Beth couldn't control her response to Jake, and wasn't sure if she liked it. "What's on your mind?"

"A walk. Tonight after dinner. What do you think?"

"Fine with me."

"Great. I'll come by your cabin."

She looked beyond him to where Wyatt, Virgil, Barrel, and a few other ranch hands talked. "What's going on with them?"

"Barrel found a dead animal. He's certain it's from the wild dog pack. He also believes it's infected with rabies."

"Where?"

"A hundred yards from the corral behind them. We're waiting for Doc Worrel and the game warden to arrive and confirm. If he's right, the pack is creating a serious threat to those on the ranch."

Her gaze narrowed on the men. "Isn't it strange they stay so close to one particular place? I thought packs traveled."

"Virgil believes it's due to the rabies, which affects their brains and how an animal acts. This one may have wandered a good distance from the pack. We won't know until Virgil gets a look at the area around the dead dog."

Beth didn't like the implications. "Are you going with them?"

"I am. We need a few men with rifles in the off chance the pack is close by while the doc and warden check the body. I'd better get going. I'll see you this evening."

Watching him walk back to the group of men, a chill slid through her. She'd never heard of animals sticking to one location. They tended to roam in a quest for food. Their den had to be close to the ranch. If so, why hadn't the numerous searches found it?

"Are you ready?" Jake leaned against the front doorjamb of Beth's cabin as she slipped on her heavy coat. A few feet away, Duke panted, ready for the humans to get moving.

"I am." Closing the door, she moved past him, somewhat surprised when he reached out to lace his fingers with hers. Warmth spread through her. "What did you find out this afternoon?"

He knew what she referred to. "The dead animal was one of the wild dogs." His gaze swept to Duke, glad they'd been able to save him from the pack.

"How could they tell it wasn't someone's pet?"

"Condition of the teeth, coat, claws, and no collar. According to Doc Worrel, almost a hundred percent of dog owners buy collars, many with small metal name tags attached. Her guess is he wandered away from the pack, got lost, and died from lack of food and dehydration."

Considering his explanation, she glanced toward where the animal had been found. "Is there another search planned?"

"The game warden is organizing one. I don't plan to be a part of it unless Virgil wants me to. There's a lot of work to do around here. We're getting ready to build the additional cabins not long after Christmas. The days will move quickly once construction starts. How did your meeting with Margie go?”

“With everything going on, I’m surprised you remembered.”

“I’m interested in everything when it comes to you, Beth.”

Feeling her face heat, she looked away. “Other than a couple changes, she approved the menu. The invitations were mailed today. Honestly, I’m a little nervous.”

Squeezing her hand, he lifted it, brushing a kiss across the knuckles. “You’re a pro at this. They’re going to love whatever you do.”

Lowering their joined hands, his phone rang. The caller was someone he couldn’t ignore. “Excuse me a minute.” Letting go of her hand, he answered. “Hey, Dillon.”

“Evening, Jake. Am I interrupting anything?”

“I’ve got a few minutes. What’s on your mind?”

“I called your doctor. He confirmed you’re good to compete this coming season. Are you still interested?”

Jake glanced at Beth, knowing what happened next would impact their budding relationship. “I’m interested enough to get your input on my chances.”

“You’ve gotta be all in on this, Jake.”

“What are you thinking?”

“Same events as before. I’ll send you the schedule. Estimated start is March. What do you think?”

A month ago, he would’ve jumped at this chance. Now... “Send me the schedule, Dillon. I have some commitments here I need to finish." Jake watched as Beth knelt to pet Duke.

"Right now, I need to know if I can count on you. Yes or no?"

Glancing down at Beth once more, their gazes locked. "Yes."

Chapter Eighteen

Beth didn't ask about the phone call, though something about it had her stomach churning. The way Jake looked at her while on the phone held a meaning she couldn't decipher. She decided not to ask. If he wanted to share what was said, he would.

Jake spoke little during the remainder of their walk. When she'd dared a glance, he stared straight ahead, lost in thought. Beth knew it had to do with the call.

"That was Dillon, my agent."

Her brows drew together. "Agent?"

"Rodeo agent. Before my last injury, Dillon handled all my publicity, including television appearances, interviews with magazines and newspapers, creating and ordering merchandise, finding sponsorship opportunities, and negotiating my contracts."

"I had no idea."

"Most people don't. Even with my injury, I still have a couple open sponsorships. The merchandise still sells through my website, and I'm pretty sure Dillon is lining up interviews and appearances for me. The man is a machine when it comes to his talent."

"Talent would be you?"

Chuckling, he squeezed her hand. "Me and a few other rodeo athletes."

"So the call was Dillon checking in with you."

Pursing his lips, he shook his head. "Not quite. He's pushing me to start competing again in March."

Heart thudding in her chest, she felt sick. "March. As in three months?"

"Yes."

"What did you tell him?"

"I told him yes."

"Oh…" There didn't seem to be much else to say.

The sound of her flat voice was a punch to Jake's gut. What did he expect? She, like Wyatt and Virgil, expected him to stay until at least October of next year. One full dude ranch season. They'd hired him for just that purpose. And because his best friend, Trace, had assured them Jake would do a terrific job.

Guilt ate at him. Not being upfront with people had never been his way. Jake regarded himself as honest, a person others could trust. The answer he'd given Dillon to his question about rejoining the rodeo didn't portray him as either upfront or honest.

Beth's thoughts were on Jake the following morning as she made several changes Margie requested to the menu. Not so much changes as eliminating one of the main dishes and adding another dessert. Both were made to accommodate Anson's tastes, Margie had confided before they'd wrapped up their meeting the previous afternoon.

Tucking one copy of the menu into her file, she set another one on Margie's desk. Glancing around the beautiful office before leaving, she spotted an open window. Odd, as the temperature hovered around twenty degrees.

Crossing the room, she reached up to close the window when she heard a whining sound from outside. Looking outside, Beth's heart constricted at finding Duke huddled against the outside wall of the lodge.

Closing the window, she hurried to the shivering dog. It had been a while since they'd found what turned out to be a beautiful golden Labrador retriever. Doc Worrel had announced him healthy, and sent him back to the ranch with Jake. They'd posted flyers, hoping to locate his owner, and Margie had taken out a short ad in the local paper. As far as Beth knew, no one had responded.

"What are you doing out here, Duke? You have a beautiful spot in the barn."

After the previous ranch dog, Trooper, had left with Koa, she knew the men had adopted Duke. Even so, Duke saw Jake as his master, not staying too far away while he worked.

Standing, she glanced around. "Where's Jake?"

This got Duke's attention. Jumping up, he ran several paces toward the barn, then turned back toward her.

"All right. Let's go to the barn." Partway there, a cold chill raced through Beth. It reminded her all she wore was a heavy sweater without a coat. "Real smart," she muttered, following Duke inside the cavernous building.

Duke spotted Jake right away at the far end. Racing toward him, the lab danced around the small group of men before plopping down at Jake's feet. Leaning down, he absently stroked the dog's head, not noticing Beth watching him. When he did, she'd already turned around to hurry back to the lodge.

"What do you think, Jake?"

Straightening, he returned to the conversation with Brady. Virgil's younger cousin had been designated as Jake's assistant in constructing the new cabins.

"No reason to lay out the cabins before the first of the year. They'll be the same as the others."

"Virgil said two will be bigger," Brady reminded him.

"He mentioned that to me. They'll be located closest to the lodge. Let's head outside."

Brady walked beside Jake, through the deepening snow, as they closed in on the spot where the large cabins would be built.

"Virgil told me you had construction experience."

Brady shrugged. "My best friend's father owns a construction firm. Mostly new homes and remodels. I worked summers for him since turning fourteen, then full-time after high school. Learned a lot. Then Virgil called, and I decided to give it a try."

"You never worked on a ranch before?"

"I helped out some older cousins on their place after school. Mainly mucked stalls, exercised horses, cleaned tack, and sometimes worked with the cattle. They did let me ride whenever I wanted." He grinned. "That was the best part. I would've worked for free in order to ride."

"I know what you mean."

"Virgil told me you used to rodeo. He said you were real good. Ever thought of going back?"

The question surprised Jake. Instead of answering, he offered a shrug.

"Right here is where one of the larger cabins will be built. Twenty to twenty-five feet away will be the second one. My understanding is they're meant for larger families. I suppose two couples could share one. Each has one bathroom and mini kitchen, the same as the smaller cabins. Have you seen the blueprints?"

"Virgil showed them to me. I suggested they consider changing the large ones to two-story. They could add a loft. Just a thought."

"I'll talk to Virgil about it." Jake's thoughts moved to Beth, and how a large cabin with loft would be perfect for the two of them. His breath caught, wondering where the idea had come from.

"How many smaller cabins are going to be built?"

"We've been talking about five smaller, plus the two larger. They originally planned for this number, so the septic system was designed for it."

"So, after these seven new cabins, there won't be any more built?" Brady turned to face the existing cabins.

"That's my understanding."

Both men glanced toward the parking area at the rumbling truck engine. The white Chevy three-quarter ton parked next to Anson's truck. Two men climbed out.

"Haven't seen them out here in a while. Come on. I'll introduce you to Wyatt's brothers."

Brady's eyes flashed for an instant. "Brothers?"

"Yep. Wyatt's the oldest. Jonah is the next oldest. Has an MBA and law degree, and handles all the business needs of the ranch. Gage is the youngest. His degree is in recreation and tourism. He's real involved with activities for the guests. They took off after the end of last season to visit other dude ranches. I think they covered five states."

Meeting the brothers outside the lodge, Jake held out his hand. "Jonah. Gage. It's good to see you. This is Virgil's cousin, Brady. He's been here a few weeks."

After greetings, Jake nodded toward the cabins. "We've been talking about the cabins that'll be built after the first of the year. Brady did construction for several years."

"Yeah?" Gage asked, seeing the ranch hand's slight nod. "We did okay with the first round, but it would be good to have someone with more experience."

"We acted as our own contractor the last time," Jonah explained. "We hired out the plumbing and electrical work. Have you done either of those, Brady?"

"A lot of plumbing, but not much electrical." His features twisted. "Before you ask, I've got no interest in learning more. I hate getting shocked."

The three laughed, Jonah clasping him on the shoulder. "I don't blame you. We'd better get inside before Mom comes charging out. Good to meet you, Brady."

Gage lifted his chin at Brady before following Jonah inside.

"Wyatt told me they share a house at the north end of town, but stay in the lodge if the weather's bad. Jonah's planning to build something on the ranch next year."

"What about Gage?" Brady asked as they headed back toward the barn.

"No idea. They own the house in town, so he'll probably stay there. Virgil mentioned him being a volunteer firefighter and smoke jumper. Of the three brothers, he has the most outside interests."

"How about you, Jake?"

"What do you mean?"

"What do you do when you're not working at the ranch?"

He'd never thought much about other interests. His life had evolved around the rodeo, the same as most of his friends who competed.

"Good question. I'll have to give it some thought."

Which is what he did much of the rest of the day. Jake enjoyed reading, played some online games to relax, and at one time, liked to cook. With all the meals being provided as part of his job, he couldn't recall the last time he'd made his mother's lasagna, or his father's barbecued tri-tip.

It had been a while since he'd gone dancing, since at least his rodeo days. Anyway, he didn't believe that counted.

He'd enjoyed fishing when younger, though it had been a long time since he'd held a rod. Jake had heard Gage was a heckuva fisherman. Maybe he'd talk to him about getting back into it, or perhaps rock climbing, at which Gage excelled.

He could speak with Beth, find out what she did to relax. Probably cook, he chuckled to himself.

The ideas kept flowing as he finished his chores for the day. Surprisingly, not one of them involved the rodeo.

Chapter Nineteen

Beth slid the phone into her pocket, glad her mother hadn't heard the call. This one had been from her brother, Julian.

The executive who'd been fired due to unethical actions had called to apologize. Not for his actions, but for the actions of someone else. He'd learned his wife had made threatening calls to Julian and Beth.

Hoping his old boss wouldn't pursue legal action, he'd assured Julian that his wife would never call them again. She'd been devastated when he'd lost his job, taking it out on Julian and Beth.

For their part, Julian and Beth were glad the mystery had ended. Now they could move on without the stress of the harassing calls.

"Beth, would you mind bringing out the pitcher of tea?" Donna Jenner relaxed in a chair at her dining room table, waiting for her daughter to serve the pie. She'd made coconut cream, Beth's favorite. Donna wondered if that had changed since she was a teenager.

"This looks delicious, Mom." She set the plates holding oversized slices of pie on the table before returning to the kitchen for the tea. Filling their glasses, she sat down, anxious to taste what she knew would be delicious pie.

"What have you been doing since I saw you at Thanksgiving?" Donna sipped tea, waiting for Beth to give her opinion of the dessert.

"This is fabulous, Mom. Best ever."

A laugh burst from Donna's throat. "You say that each time I make it."

Beth smiled. "It's true."

"All right. Is Margie keeping you busy?"

"Always. She's decided to throw a dinner party in a couple weeks for about thirty people. The invitations were mailed yesterday."

"My guess is she asked you to create a new menu." Donna slid a forkful of pie into her mouth.

"Good guess. I'm actually excited to prepare a more upscale meal than the dinners for the ranch hands."

"The boys I spoke with love your cooking."

"I admit to cooking a mean roast."

"You know what I mean. Tell me what you'll be making."

Setting down her fork, lips twisting as she pictured the menu. "Let's see. Fennel-crusted roast pork with vegetables, steak au poivre, shrimp and orzo, honey and balsamic glazed salmon, roasted tomatoes with marinated feta, crispy carrot latkes, vegetable torte, and vanilla-roasted sweet potatoes. Plus assorted appetizers and desserts."

"Sounds wonderful. I'm assuming Abigail will help you."

"I couldn't do it without her. I'm so glad Jake mentioned hiring her."

"How is she doing?"

A brow lifting, Beth's head tilted to the side. "What do you mean?"

"You must have noticed Abigail is dealing with something difficult. The poor girl doesn't smile. I never spotted a single one during my stay."

Thinking back on the day Abigail arrived at the ranch, Beth remembered thinking the same. The younger woman carried a burden, something she had chosen not to share. Beth wondered if she'd confided in Jake.

"Abigail hasn't said anything to me."

"You've noticed, though, right?"

"Yes, I have. I'm hoping she's spoken to Jake about whatever troubles her."

Picking up her glass, Donna sipped more tea. "She works for you. Why don't you ask her yourself?"

"I don't know if that's a good idea. If she shuts me out, it could put a wedge between us."

"You're probably right." Picking up her plate and glass, Donna took them to the kitchen sink, sensing Beth right behind her. "I'm sure she'll say something when she's ready."

Maybe, Beth thought. *Maybe she will.*

Jake tightened the jacket's collar around his neck, ducking his head against the snow slamming against his face. The storm had blown in overnight, covering the ground in almost a foot of fresh snow.

This was not what he hoped for on Saturday morning. Other than quick greetings, he hadn't spoken to Beth in a few days. Abigail had told him she'd visited her mother the day before.

His mind had continued to whirl with questions about his future, what was right for him and for the ranch. Could he be gone a few months and keep his job? The only way to know would be to speak with Virgil and Wyatt, and he wasn't ready to walk down that path.

The force of the storm had increased by the time he reached the barn. Checking the small stall Duke called home, he was surprised to find the lab huddled in a corner.

"Duke, you lazy bum." Kneeling down, he stroked the dog's head. "Wish I was still hunkered down in bed." When he stood, so did Duke. "Come on, boy. Let's see if Beth is in the kitchen. Bet she'll have something for you."

Even with the deepening snow, Duke bounded toward the lodge. Reaching the back door, he sat down and barked. When the door inched open to show Beth on the other side, he barked again.

"Good morning, Duke. Hello, Jake. Hold on a minute." She closed the door to keep out the snow. Picking up a piece of turkey, she opened the door just enough to hand it outside. "Here you go, boy. Wish I could let you in the kitchen, but…" She gave a slight shrug, along with a crooked grin.

"Are we still on for dinner tonight?" He hoped she hadn't changed her mind.

"I'm looking forward to it. Assuming the roads are clear. I'd better get back to finishing breakfast for the men. See you later, Jake."

"Definitely."

Closing the door, she leaned against it for a moment, garnering a curious look from Abigail. "Jake stopped by with a hungry Duke."

"Ah. I see." The tiniest of grins accompanied the knowing look.

Feeling her face heat, she went back to work without further comment. When Jake arrived with the other men for breakfast, she asked Abigail to deliver the food to the dining room, creating a decent distance between her and Jake.

She didn't want others to make similar conclusions about the two of them. Later, she realized how silly the efforts were. Anyone who'd witnessed their evening walks already knew they were becoming close friends. Maybe more.

Taking one last look in the mirror, Beth sighed in resignation. The jeans were clean, and the sweater a pretty shade of pink. Matched with the black and pink knit scarf and black boots, it was a nice, chic look. Then why did she feel so frumpy?

Because you're overthinking the dinner date with Jake, she told herself.

Taking several deep breaths, she stretched her arms up, then out to the sides in an attempt to relax. Beth hoped as soon as he arrived, the tension would vanish.

The storm had continued throughout the day without dumping too much more snow on the ground. Temperatures had hovered around twenty-five and were expected to lower further.

Selecting her warmest coat, she pulled a pair of dressier gloves from the dresser drawer, along with a knit cap. Placing those by the door, she sat down, then stood, then sat down again.

"This is silly," she muttered, annoyed at her nervous energy. "It's just a date."

For some unfathomable reason, it felt like more. As if she were at a critical juncture in her life, and Jake was the key to the future.

"Not if he leaves for the rodeo." Saying the words aloud made them more real. She had to remember he might not stay at the ranch. If he left, the odds were he'd never return.

What about her future? Beth hadn't spent much time considering how long she'd stay at Whistle Rock Ranch. She enjoyed the work, even if it wasn't overly challenging. Feed the men lots of good food and they were happy.

Coupled with planning a few of Margie's dinner parties, and Beth could see staying for quite a while.

She startled at the strident raps on the door. Standing, she opened the door, aware of how the nervous tension had evaporated.

"Good evening, Beth."

"Hello, Jake. Come in while I get my coat."

He stepped closer. "Let me help you." Holding it up, she slipped into the heavy coat before putting on her hat and gloves.

"I'm ready."

"Great. The roads have been cleared, and the storm appears to have moved on." He grasped her hand as they stepped off the porch.

"It's beautiful." She gazed upward at the clear sky covered with brilliant stars.

"Yes, it is." Though he wasn't talking about the sky. He hadn't taken his gaze off her since entering the cabin. Beth was the most beautiful woman he'd ever seen.

When they reached the truck, he opened the passenger door, assisting her into the seat. Adjusting the seat belt, she relaxed, more than ready for an evening with Jake.

"Where are we going?"

"A new place Wyatt told me about. He and Daisy ate there before Thanksgiving."

"Sounds perfect. What's the name of the restaurant?"

"Uh...I don't recall."

She cocked a brow. "Um..."

"No worries." He flashed her a smile. "Wyatt told me how to get there."

It took little time to reach an enchanting Victorian home. There were two stories, and even though snow covered the garden and roof, Beth could make out yellow paint, white trim, and deep blue-green shutters.

"Chez Rémy," Beth read out loud. "This is amazing. I can't wait to see the menu."

"Wyatt mentioned the problem is the parking. They don't have any. We'll find a place on the street."

Beth pointed to a large opening. "There's a big one across the street."

Parking, he rushed around the truck to help Beth to the ground. He took her arm, slipping it through his.

"Watch for ice." He warned her twice. Once crossing the street and again taking the steps to the entry.

"Oh, my gosh. This is fabulous." Beth didn't remove her coat before walking into the dining room to take a slow turn. "Absolutely brilliant."

"Uh, Beth?" He nodded toward the hostess.

"Oh, sorry."

"Good evening. Do you have a reservation?"

Beth bit back a response. At least eighty percent of the tables were empty.

"Yes, ma'am. Jake Kelman."

"And it's just you two?"

"Just us, ma'am."

"We have a wonderful table in a quiet spot by the window." Retrieving menus, she walked them to the perfect spot for their date. "Will this do?"

"It's great. Thank you." He pulled out Beth's chair, taking the one next to her for himself.

Picking up a pitcher at a nearby cart, the hostess filled their glasses. "Would you care for anything else to drink?"

Beth tore her gaze from the menu to look up. "I'd like hot tea."

"And you, sir?"

"Coffee, please."

As the hostess walked off, Beth could no longer contain her excitement. "This menu is incredible. I want to try everything."

"Then we'll have to return every week."

She laughed, then looked into his eyes. Jake meant every word.

Chapter Twenty

Beth couldn't have been more impressed with her meal, or with his. Jake had chuckled each time she reached over to stab a piece of meat, a vegetable, or the magnificent risotto. All with his permission, of course.

"I cannot eat another bite."

"What about dessert, Beth?"

A tentative grin formed. "If we can put it off for a bit, then I'd love to try one of them."

"Maybe they'll fix you a sampler." He sipped his third cup of coffee.

"Not a bad idea. I'll ask." She leaned forward, lowering her voice. "Is everything all right with Abigail?"

His features tensed. "What do you mean?"

Stirring her tea, she tasted it, adding a touch of cream. "First, her work is great. I couldn't function without her."

"That's the main thing, right?"

"Yes, it is. I'm more worried than anything."

"What worries you, Beth?"

"This may sound silly, but I've never seen her smile. Not once since she arrived, Jake. She often seems down. To be clear, I'm not saying I believe she's depressed."

"Are you interested in dessert?" The server had arrived without either noticing.

"We'd love to see the menu."

"There isn't a menu, as there are only five choices, ma'am."

Beth shot a look at Jake, who nodded. "What are the choices?"

Listing them, the server answered questions, then waited.

"I'll have the fresh peach cobbler," Jake said.

"They all sound wonderful. Is there any chance you offer a sampler?"

"This is the first time anyone has asked. I'll check with the chef and be right back."

The server returned with a broad smile. "We can prepare a special plate for you with four of five desserts. The Crème Brulé can be split. The portions will be very small. One bite each. Would that be acceptable?"

"Perfect. Thank you for checking."

"Yes, ma'am. I'll be back with your desserts."

Beth waited until the server brought dessert before continuing their conversation. "My guess is something happened, which continues to burden her." She took a taste of chocolate ganache. "Oh my. This is wonderful. Try some."

He held up his hand. "I have plenty here." Jake scooped up a large bite of cobbler. Swallowing, he looked at Beth. "I agree about Abbie. Something had to have happened or she never would've moved down here."

"The end of a relationship?"

Jake shook his head. "I just don't know. We were real close before I left to rodeo. It's been years since we've spent much time together."

"Then her being here is a blessing for both of you."

"But you're worried. Do you think she might do something serious?"

"Such as, hurt herself? Not at all. It's as if a dark cloud follows her around. Do you think she'd open up to you?"

Jake's mouth drew into a thin line. "I just don't know. The hardest part is figuring out how to approach her. Getting her off the ranch might help."

"Christmas is coming up. Maybe ask if she'd join you to shop."

"Shop?" He threw back his head and laughed. "She'd know right away something was up." Finishing his cobbler, he swallowed the last of his coffee. "I'll think of something."

Jake hadn't intended to spend their evening talking about his sister. He wanted to learn more about Beth, what she does for fun, and her plans for the future.

"Tell me what you like to do when you aren't cooking."

"Or visiting my mother?"

He chuckled. "Yeah."

Sucking in a slow breath, she released it, thinking about activities during her free time. A few minutes ticked by before she met his expectant gaze.

"Gosh, I'm not certain. Sometimes, I cook recipes that will never be served at the ranch."

"I'm not sure that counts since you're a chef by profession."

"Maybe it doesn't. What else?" She tapped fingers on the table, her mouth twisting in concentration. "I enjoy reading and traveling. Though I don't have much time for either."

A smile tipped up the corners of her mouth. "Mom taught me how to sew. I used to love creating pillows, curtains, and tablecloths for our house. There aren't as many fabric stores as there used to be. Most people end up buying online. Oh, and I used to play softball."

That seemed to surprise Jake.

"I played through high school. Our team did pretty good. We made it through the state semi-finals, but didn't make it to the finals."

"What position did you play?"

"Second base, and sometimes first base. I loved it." A wistful expression remained as she thought back on her high school days. "What about you, Jake?"

"I don't have interests beyond working. There isn't time to fit more into each day."

"What about the rodeo?"

"It's not a hobby, Beth. As much as I loved it, the rodeo was my job. Competing became a way of life. Trace and I competed together until he decided to get his family back. Before then, we both did real well in the rodeo."

"Then you were injured."

"Right." He thought of the ride, flying into the air, tumbling to the ground, and the audible crack when he landed. "I'd already made enough points to be in the money for the season, but I couldn't compete the last season."

"Are you physically able to compete now?" She poured another cup of tea, adding cream and stirring.

"The doctor approved my return. His okay was the last hurdle."

"When will you tell Wyatt and Virgil you'll be leaving?"

Reaching out, he covered her hand with his. "I haven't made up my mind, Beth. There's a lot to consider."

She found it hard to swallow the soothing tea. Instead of commenting, she nodded.

"You have to understand, the rodeo to me has been what being a chef is to you. The thought of never being a part of it again..." Jake shook his head, looking past her to an old painting of a cowboy and his horse.

"All right. So there's the rodeo. Assuming you had extra time, what else would you do?"

Removing his hand from hers, he thought a moment. "Fish. It's been years since I held a pole. Virgil told me there are a lot of good places right on the ranch. I'd also like to try rock climbing. Gage Bonner is supposed to be an expert. Maybe I can get pointers from him."

"I'm sure he'll be your guide when the snow melts."

Finishing the last drop of coffee, he thought of something else. "I used to play baseball."

Her eyes brightened. "You did?"

"Absolutely. Like most kids, I started in elementary school and continued through junior high. Best hitter on the team."

Chuckling, she clasped her hands together on the top of the table. "What position did you play?"

"Outfield. Usually right, but we moved around. I even played catcher when ours was out."

"Do you still have your glove?"

"It's packed away somewhere. What about you?"

"It's in a box in my mother's attic. I'll have to remember to look for it during my next visit."

"Someday, we'll have to play catch. Maybe…"

The waiter approached, stopping whatever else Jake meant to say. "Will there be anything else?"

"We're finished," Jake answered.

"Thank you for coming. We hope you'll dine with us again."

You can count on it, Jake thought while admiring the woman next to him.

Jake had a great deal to think about. Spending time with Beth confirmed how much he enjoyed her company. There'd never been a woman he could see spending the rest of his life getting to know. Beth filled the role, and more.

If he just didn't have the dream of the rodeo hanging over him…

Jake had allowed competing to become his life. Not a hobby, not a job, but an overwhelming presence which owned every minute of his time. If he hadn't been injured, it would've continued to control him. Home had become the site of the next rodeo.

Whistle Rock Ranch opened possibilities he'd never considered. Yes, someday he would've met the right woman, married, and had children. But those days were a long way off. At least that was what he thought until meeting Beth. She'd became an unexpected and interesting complication.

Then there was the Magnus Ranch. Virgil had spoken to Wyatt, who'd spoken to his father. Anson called Seth Magnus, learning the rancher had made the decision to put the ranch up for sale in the spring. They'd talked numbers, discussed a few other matters, then Anson reported what he'd learned to Wyatt.

Bottom line was Jake could afford to buy the ranch and have plenty of capital left to operate it. Anson had assured Jake the Bonners weren't interested in buying Seth's land. They were in the middle of closing a deal for a huge parcel not far from Whistle Rock. It was a deal Jonah Bonner had identified and negotiated over the last couple months.

Jake knew he'd never get a better deal. Even if he couldn't work the property full time now, he could hire a foreman to operate it while he was away with the rodeo.

A call to Seth Magnus the following Monday had gone well. They'd made a verbal agreement, one allowing Jake to take over ownership on January first. Seth would remain in the house and operate the ranch for six more months, allowing Jake time to locate a foreman.

For reasons he didn't quite understand, he'd mentioned none of this to Beth. He'd confided in his best friend, Trace, and planned to talk with Abigail this week.

So why not Beth?

Chapter Twenty-One

Abigail's forehead scrunched in concentration as she assembled the cheese and mushroom raviolis planned for dinner. The recipe had been given to her by the owner of a restaurant in Sheridan, Wyoming.

When Beth announced they'd be offering a night of Italian cuisine, Abigail had pulled it from her personal journal. A wave of excitement raced through her when Beth gave her approval. Besides her position at Whistle Rock, the decision had given Abigail the first reason to celebrate in a long time.

"What are you preparing?"

Lifting her head at the familiar voice, she nodded at her brother. "Raviolis. Beth has planned a night of Italian food for dinner."

"Yeah?" Jake moved closer, scrutinizing how she filled the pasta with just the right amount of the cheese and mushroom mixture before sealing the ravioli. "Can I try?"

Her head whipped upward so she could look into his eyes. "You want to learn how to make ravioli?"

"If you have time to show me."

Studying him for a moment, she shrugged. "Wash your hands and put on an apron."

Tying the apron around him before washing his hands, he took a place next to Abigail. "Okay. Show me what to do."

"First, don't rush. It may be awkward at first, especially with your big hands. Now, watch me again, then prepare your own."

Three tries later, he produced a ravioli both of them approved. When the pile reached ten, he stepped back, satisfied with his accomplishment.

"Thanks, Abbie. I enjoyed that."

"You did real well, Jake. Better than I expected." Her eyes flashed with mischief. "Stop by anytime if you want to learn more."

"I may just do that." Removing the apron, he turned to find Beth standing off to the side with an amused expression. "Hey. I didn't know you were here."

"I've been watching for a few minutes. You did very well." She crossed the room to stand next to him. "We're having Mexican food night tomorrow. Stop by if you want to learn how to make enchiladas."

Brushing a quick kiss across her cheek, he thanked Abigail before stepping outside. Leaning back inside, he grinned. "I may just do that. I've been curious about the secret to your special enchiladas."

Touching her cheek, she shivered at the warm skin where he'd kissed her. "Well, um...what else needs to be prepared for tonight?"

Months after he'd been gravely injured, Jake believed his future had begun to fall into place. His own ranch, another shot at the rodeo, and maybe a life with Beth.

He understood her lack of enthusiasm at him competing again. His best friend, Trace, who never thought he'd leave the rodeo, warned Jake about competing again. His leg may be healed but would always be weak. Another injury could result in losing his ability to walk, or worse.

Did he want to take the chance?

The question haunted him the rest of the day and on his walk to the lodge for dinner. Not until he sat down between Brady and Barrel did he recall making some of tonight's ravioli.

Studying the stuffed, round pasta with a crimped edge, he thought it easy to pick out a few of his masterpieces. They were a little more oval, and more plump than the others. He scooped them onto his plate before selecting alfredo sauce. By the time he added a large square of meat lasagna, and crusty garlic bread, his plate was full. His stomach growled when he sat back down.

"Hungry?" Brady chuckled as he placed a forkful of the lasagna into his mouth.

"Starving." Jake tried the ravioli first, loving the mix of flavors. "This is great." He pointed at his plate with the tongs of his fork.

"Beth's food is always great."

"Yes, it is." Glancing up, Jake's gaze locked on Beth. She stood at the door into the kitchen, scanning the buffet table for empty serving dishes.

They had an unspoken agreement not to make too much of their relationship in front of the ranch hands. This didn't include their evening walks or dinner in town. Those were theirs to share, no matter who happened to see them.

Catching her attention, he gave a slight chin lift. In return, she sent him a slight smile.

Jake slowed his pace, finishing as the others left the lodge. Picking up his plate, he carried it to the kitchen, where his sister scraped dishes and Beth wrapped leftovers. She lifted her head as he handed his plate to Abigail.

"I'll come by your cabin in an hour. Does that give you enough time?"

Beth's gaze darted to Abigail, then to Jake. "Perfect."

After a sharp nod, he left the lodge.

"Wow. I've never seen my brother like this."

Beth cleared her throat. "Like what?"

"Oh, come on. He's at least halfway in love with you."

She shook her head on a nervous chuckle. "We're friends, Abigail."

"Who hold hands and take long walks. Oh, and have intimate dinners in town. Are you blushing?"

Beth picked up the containers, opening the refrigerator door. "Of course not. I'm too old to blush."

"Ha! You aren't old at all."

That's when Beth saw it. The first smile on Abigail's face since she'd arrived at Whistle Rock. The teasing was worth enduring when it brought a bit of joy to Jake's sister.

Then Abigail's features grew serious. "Please don't hurt him."

"Me hurt Jake? I do believe it will be the other way around."

"I don't know. He's pretty into you, Beth."

She couldn't say anything to Abigail about his plans to return to the rodeo. If she didn't already know, Jake had to be the one to tell her. Beth wondered if his leaving would stun Abigail as much as it had surprised her.

The smart move would be for Beth to put distance between her and Jake. She couldn't speak for him, but there was little doubt she'd fallen in love with the lanky cowboy.

She recalled how dejected she'd been when Freddie ended their relationship. Beth knew the pain would be tenfold when Jake left to rejoin the rodeo.

Once again, she'd bury herself in her work, spend more time with her mother, and find other activities to make up for their evening walks.

She doubted he'd return to Whistle Rock. Why would he? The rodeo would become his life, as it had before his injury.

Perhaps he'd pay a visit to his sister every now and then. Those times would be the hardest for Beth.

As her mother often reminded her, the Jenners were a tough family. Beth would make it, as she had every other setback in her life. She'd find a way to forget him and become stronger for the challenge.

"I can take care of everything here, Beth. Go on to your cabin and get ready for your walk."

"Thanks, Abigail. See you in the morning."

"Yeah. See you."

Closing the door behind her, Beth realized the joy had left Abigail's voice.

Slipping into his warmest coat, Jake frowned when his phone rang. Thinking it was either Virgil or Wyatt, he pulled it from a pocket.

"Hello."

"Jake?"

The breath rushed from his lungs at the familiar voice. On the other end of the line was the last person he expected.

"Helena?"

"It's me."

Frustrated, he checked the time, knowing Beth expected him any minute. "I'm leaving to meet someone. What do you want?" He winced at the sharp tone.

"I'll make this quick." There was an unexpected hesitancy in her voice. "I called to thank you."

"Thank me?"

"You were right. I have to do this on my own."

"Are you in rehab?"

"My mother found a program in Montana. I have to work to help pay the cost, which I've figured out is for the best. Guess what I'm doing?"

"I have no idea."

"Mucking stalls, exercising horses, cleaning tack. Everything I always hated."

He chuckled despite his need to get going. "After hating ranch work your entire life. Guess you've gone full circle."

She laughed. "Guess so. Anyway, I wanted to thank you. And, well...I'm sorry for stealing the money. You were right to have me arrested."

A pang of guilt squeezed his chest. "I'm glad you're getting help, Helena."

"So am I. I'll let you go. Goodbye, Jake." The call ended before he could respond.

"Wow," he breathed out. Helena always found a way to surprise him. This was the best surprise of all.

Zipping up, then closing the snaps on his coat, he stepped into a light snow. A storm was expected by morning. Tonight, he and Beth could take advantage of the brief reprieve.

So much had happened the last month. Most good, some, not so much. Excitement rolled through him whenever he thought of the Magnus Ranch. Soon, it would be the Kelman Ranch, and he'd be the owner.

Jake had spoken with Abigail for a few minutes before dinner, telling her about the purchase. She was thrilled for him. He'd emphasized there'd always be a place for her, no questions asked. Jake had walked off when tears threatened to slide down her face.

The only person left to tell was Beth. Why was he so hesitant to share the news with her? The answer hit him as he stepped onto her porch.

Knowing he'd bought the ranch, she'd expect him to stay. Beth would assume he'd no longer pursue a return to the rodeo.

Lifting his hand, he knocked twice. He had to make decisions about sharing the news of the ranch, and a possible rodeo comeback. Tonight, though, wasn't the time for either.

Chapter Twenty-Two

"Watch out, Jake!" Barrel's shout caught everyone's attention.

Glancing up, Jake saw the problem. Hundreds of pounds of snow began to slip from the barn's roof, and he was standing directly below it. Instead of jumping outward, he chose the other direction.

Plastering himself against the barn's outer wall, he heard a loud rumbling right before an incredible crash of snow hit the ground.

"You all right, Jake?" Brady stood six feet away, on the other side of a giant pile of wet snow and ice.

Heart pounding, he lifted each booted foot to shake off the slush. "Yeah. I'm fine."

As he began climbing over the mound of snow, another crash slammed into the ground.

"Doggone. It just keeps coming." Brady jumped as far back as possible, stumbling to land on his rump. Hurrying to stand, he moved farther away. "We get a two day warm spell and this is what happens. Guaranteed another freeze will be rolling in soon."

The mound in front of Jake had grown. Instead of climbing over three feet, he'd be scaling a bit more.

"Hold on, Jake. Barrel's getting the Bobcat. You'll be out of there in minutes." Brady turned to see the white and red compact tractor making its way toward them.

As Brady said, within ten minutes Jake stood, looking up at the roof. "It was time for it to shed."

"We'll be getting more soon. That's about all you can count on during a Wyoming winter." Brady left Jake to tackle the rest of his chores.

Three days had rushed by since the last walk with Beth. They were approaching Margie's dinner party, with Christmas following not far afterward.

Beth and Abigail were putting in extra hours, cooking three meals a day while preparing ahead what they could for the dinner party. They knew the party's importance to Margie. Beth wouldn't accept anything except complete perfection.

Jake wanted to see her, watching for a few minutes as she went about her work. Beth had told him during their walk she'd be putting in long days until the party. He wouldn't interrupt her or his sister.

"Jake."

He sensed the foreman coming up beside him. "Virgil."

"Margie wants the Christmas tree today or tomorrow. She plans to have it and the house decorated before the party."

"You want me to take a few men out this afternoon?"

"If you can fit it in with your other work."

"No problem. If you have no objections, I'll take Barrel, Brady, Jimmy, and Owen. We'll probably take snowmobiles."

"Good idea, except Margie wants a sixteen foot tree."

Jake took a step back, chuckling. "That does make a difference. I'll take the truck and flat trailer. Has Barrel done this before?"

"Jimmy, Owen, and Barrel have all been on tree duty. They know where to go for the best tree selection. Margie will want it to look nice all the way around."

"So not flat on one side and round on the other."

"Right. Wyatt and I will help you and the men set it up inside. Believe me, it will take all of us. We'll also bring down the decorations from the attic. Margie, Daisy, Lily, my mother, and some friends from town will decorate most of it tomorrow."

"Except they'll need men to climb the tall ladders to do the upper third," Jake said.

Virgil rubbed the back of his neck. "Don't forget the star on top."

"Who's the lucky man?"

"It used to be Anson. Now it's Wyatt, although he doesn't love the task. With Gage and Jonah back in town, Gage might do it. He loves heights." Virgil grinned.

"Let me round up the men and get going while the light is good. Any other instructions?"

"Make certain the tank is full, and fill a cooler with water and a bag with protein bars." Virgil clasped him on the shoulder. "Thanks, Jake."

Jake drove while Barrel called out directions. Jimmy, Brady, and Owen squeezed into the back seat, telling jokes and making everyone laugh.

"You'll want to go north at the fence line." Barrel pointed to the posts and smooth wire up ahead.

"Will we need to go deep into the forest to find what Margie wants?" Jake maneuvered the truck around a large pothole.

"Nah. There are big trees right on the edge. We should be able to find a good one for Margie. Okay, so keep driving along this trail. It'll narrow down up ahead, but we can still get the trailer through it. We'll be there in another ten minutes."

Jake spotted the area Barrel mentioned the instant they rounded a corner in the trail. Several dozen large pine trees rimmed the area, making the selection easier.

Jumping out of the truck, the men spread out, knowing what Margie wanted. It didn't take long before Jimmy called out he'd found one. A second later, Brady did the same. The trees were within twenty feet of each other.

The five men first checked over Jimmy's selection. All agreed it would be perfect. Then they moved to Brady's choice. They came to the same conclusion. Taking a collectible coin from his pocket, Jake glanced around the circle.

"Heads, Jimmy's tree. Tails, Brady's tree." He tossed it in the air, letting it fall to the ground.

Five men bent over to stare at the coin. Straightening, Jake made the call.

"Heads it is. Let's get what we need from the truck."

Before any of them could take a step, a series of growls froze them in their places.

"No one move," Jake said.

"Don't think that's a problem, boss." Owen's voice shook enough for the others to notice.

"How far away are the weapons?" Barrel asked.

"They're secured in the box on the trailer," Jake said. "Everyone start moving. Real slowly."

The growls continued from behind them as they inched toward the truck. Jake was the first to reach the trailer. Working fast, he pulled out their rifles and shotguns.

Loading one of the shotguns, he turned back around, lowering his voice. "I'll provide cover while the rest of you load."

The growling grew louder as the animals closed in on them. Without warning, a single animal came at them from the left, another from the right.

"Watch out!" Jake aimed at the one attacking from the right, and fired. An eerie scream came from the wild dog as it whirled in the air, landing on the ground with a pitiful whine.

Another shot rang out seconds after Jake fired, this one from Brady. A second dog dropped to the ground. This one was silent.

The other three men joined the first two, firing as the pack of wild dogs continued to run at them. It was as if they were crazed, hurling themselves directly into the path of their own destruction.

As the last dog fell to the ground, the men kept their weapons trained toward the forest. After a few minutes, Jake lowered his shotgun. The others did the same.

"Brady and Jimmy. I want you to keep vigilant, in case there are more out there."

"Sure thing, boss." Jimmy reloaded his shotgun before taking several steps away from the trailer. From out of the thick brush to his left, a dark figure flew toward him. Before he had a chance to raise the shotgun, Jimmy crashed to the ground.

Screaming, trying to fend off the attack, Jimmy fought with all he had. He didn't feel the teeth sinking into his hand a moment before the animal stilled and fell off him.

"Jimmy!" Jake dropped down beside him.

"I'm fine."

"Stay still, Jimmy." Jake pushed up the coat and shirt to get a better look at the bite. "Barrel, get the first aid kit, and a couple bottles of water. Owen, do you have service out here?"

"Zero. Did you get a sat phone from the office?"

"It's in the truck. Call Virgil. Let him know what happened. We'll need to get Jimmy to the hospital. I need you and Brady to wrap the dog in a tarp and put him on the trailer. He'll need to be tested."

"I told you I'm fine, Jake. No hospital."

Jake just nodded at Owen to do as he asked.

Barrel ran to the cab of the truck, returning with the first aid kit and water. Removing the cap, he handed the first bottle to Jake.

Flushing the area of the dog bite with the water, he emptied both bottles before drying the area. Opening a packet of antibiotic ointment, he spread a thin amount on a bandage before pressing it over the wound.

"Brady, help me get Jimmy into the back seat of the cab."

"Geez. I can walk just fine, Jake."

"Let's find out." Helping Jimmy up, Jake kept a hand on his back and one on his chest. "Ready?"

"Yeah. I'm good." He didn't even make it one step before his legs gave out. Brady rushed to help Jake hold him up.

"All right, Jimmy. We're going to get you in the truck. Owen, don't get closer, but take another look around to see if you spot more wild dogs. Then jump into the trailer. We need to get Jimmy back to the lodge."

Nodding, Owen settled the butt of the shotgun against the soft spot between his shoulder and collarbone. His father had taught him to shoot when he was seven. To this day, the shotgun was his preferred weapon.

"We're all set, Owen. Hop on up," Jake yelled.

He didn't have to be told twice.

Stopping the truck near the barn, Jake helped Jimmy step to the ground, with Brady and Barrel on either side of their injured friend.

"We'll take him to the hospital in my truck." Jake didn't see Virgil come up next to him.

"My truck's ready to go. Brady and Barrel, get him in the back seat. You guys good to go with us? Did you bring the dog?"

"Yes. Hey, Brady. Move the dog to the back of Virgil's truck."

"No problem," Brady answered while Barrel nodded.

Virgil turned to Jake. "Tell Wyatt what happened. I'll get the story from Brady and Barrel."

"I thought we'd killed the entire pack of wild dogs. Then one came out of nowhere and took down Jimmy." He scrubbed a hand down his face. "We killed the dog, but not before it bit Jimmy's hand."

"We'll get him checked over. You did good. Thanks, Jake." Virgil rushed to his truck.

As he watched Virgil and the boys drive off, Jake felt a heavy weight pinch his chest. It would be a long time before he forgot the fear in Jimmy's eyes.

Virgil was wrong. He didn't do anything close to a good job, and he certainly didn't deserve the foreman's thanks.

Chapter Twenty-Three

Jake sat on the edge of his bed, waiting until the shakes subsided. They'd claimed him as soon as he entered his cabin, and so far, shown no signs of receding.

He'd seen severe, life-changing injuries, and even a death, during his days with the rodeo. They'd never affected him this way.

Something about the fear in Jimmy's eyes had shaken Jake. The dog had shot out of the bushes at the young ranch hand, pinning him to the ground. There hadn't been time to raise the shotgun or even turn away. The bite on Jimmy's hand had rendered it useless for defending against the animal.

Jake knew they'd killed the dog and pulled him off Jimmy in less than a minute. A lot could happen in sixty seconds, as Jake knew from personal experience.

Shoving up from the bed, he crossed the hall to the small bathroom. A hot shower might help calm the jitters, and maybe even restore the appetite lost when the dogs attacked.

Washing up, he let the hot water stream over his head and down his back. The tension began seeping down the drain with the suds and water. By the time he dried himself and dressed, Jake sensed a return to normal. Even the hunger he'd lost growled its presence.

Checking the time, he pulled on his boots before grabbing his coat and hat. If he hurried, he'd make the last half of dinner.

The storm had come on strong while he'd been shuttered inside. He shivered as he tugged the coat around him. This time, they were shivers from the cold, not his reaction at the attack.

Finding an open spot between a couple of newer ranch hands, he grabbed the plate and filled it with tonight's venison roast, potatoes, carrots, and Abigail's magnificent gravy. Spotting slices of Beth's dark chocolate cake, he snapped up a piece before they disappeared.

He spoke little while eating, preferring to keep silent while listening to the banter around him. Checking the other tables, he noted Virgil, Brady, Barrel, and Jimmy hadn't returned from the hospital.

Jake wondered what the hospital tests had found. The worst news would be the transmittal of rabies. For that, they'd need to wait for test results on the dog.

Similar to other nights, he waited until the others finished and left the dining room. Rising, he took his plates toward the kitchen. Beth came to him the instant he stepped inside, taking the plates from him.

"You're all right?"

He set his hands on her shoulders. "I'm fine, Beth." His gaze moved to Abigail, whose tense expression eased.

"What happened? All we saw was Brady and Barrel help Jimmy into Virgil's truck. Abigail and I assumed they were taking him to the hospital."

Jake explained about their search for a Christmas tree, the wild dog pack attacking them, and what happened to Jimmy.

"They'll do tests on Jimmy and the dog. From the time we heard the dogs growling to us killing the last dog, couldn't have been more than five minutes." Seeing the distress on Beth's face, he ran fingers down her cheek. "It could've been much worse."

Beth stepped away. "I know. When will we know anything about Jimmy?"

The sound of voices outside the kitchen's back door preceded three men entering. Virgil, Brady, and Barrel stopped to remove their jackets.

"Any food left, Beth?" Virgil hung his coat on a hook.

"Plenty. How's Jimmy?"

Resting hands on his hips, Virgil shook his head. "They're keeping him for at least one night. Maybe longer. The bites to his left hand may require surgery. A doctor from Jackson will be there tomorrow to give his opinion."

"Any news on the dog?"

Virgil knew what Jake asked. "Doc Worrel can't find any trace of rabies. She's sent tests off and asked for a rush on the results. The local warden will head out tomorrow to pick up the other carcasses for testing. I'd like you to go with him, Jake."

"No problem. Grab dinner. I'll sit down with you so we can talk more."

Jake stretched out on his bed hours later, staring at the ceiling. The events of the day, as well as those of the last few weeks, played through his mind.

Jimmy in the hospital, with the possibility of facing painful injections for rabies, ate at him. Recalling the trip to find the perfect tree for Margie, he sought answers to what he could've done to prevent the attack and Jimmy's injury.

What were the odds the dog pack would've still been on ranch property?

Odds didn't matter any longer. The outcome of their trip had been one man in the hospital. Not an acceptable result under any circumstances.

Forgetting sleep, he went to the cabin's mini kitchen. If he couldn't sleep, he might as well brew a mug of coffee.

There was still so much to consider. Purchasing the Magnus Ranch had been somewhat impulsive, yet he held no remorse. The property and existing angus cattle operation were perfect. Prime beef which sold to upscale restaurants.

Jake planned additional research on the ultra-prime Black Wagyu breed. They'd have to be raised in a separate area under conditions optimal to that breed of cattle. For the near future, the existing operation would provide the income required to run the ranch.

Sliding the pad of paper and pen toward him, he jotted a few notes about the ranch, and questions to ask Seth. As far as Jake knew, the only people who knew about the sale were him, Seth, the Bonner family, Abigail, and Virgil.

Telling Beth would be tricky. She'd expect him to forget about the rodeo, and he wasn't sure he could give up that dream.

An idea came to him. He considered it for quite a while, looking at it from all angles. There were several moving pieces, requiring numerous phone calls, hoping his contacts would come through.

The idea felt right. Grinning, he realized it might be the answer he'd been seeking. Making another note, he shoved the paper away, setting the pen aside.

Heading back to bed, he closed his eyes. This time, sleep captured him within minutes.

Jake, Barrel, Owen, and Brady drove to the site of the animal attack the following morning. The trailer was again hitched to the truck. The local game warden drove behind them, with a deputy sheriff in the seat beside him.

The weather had cleared, making it easier to locate the downed animals. It had been no more than sixteen hours since they'd left the scene, yet most of the carcasses had already been picked over.

The warden took pictures, writing down the men's account of the attack. Everyone helped load the dead animals onto the bed of the warden's truck before he and the deputy left for town. After cutting down the tree and loading it onto the trailer, the men made their way back to the ranch. Everything took less than two hours.

Their arrival drew the attention of the remaining ranch hands, as well as Margie, Anson, Beth, and Abigail. It took eight men to carry the tree inside. The main room at the lodge had been prepared the previous day, with all the tables, lamps, chairs, and other furniture moved out of the way. Anything which might hinder raising the tree and securing it.

Wyatt had taken charge, directing the men while making sure everyone else stood a safe distance away. Once the tree was up and secured, he let the men return to their jobs so Margie and her friends could start decorating. If all went well, the tree could still be ready before dinner.

"Thank you, Jake. The tree is perfect."

"Thank you, ma'am, but all of us selected it. Actually, Jimmy was the one who pointed it out."

Margie let out a breath, shaking her head. "Jimmy. He's such a good young man. I hope they release him from the hospital soon."

"Yes, ma'am." When Jake's phone rang, he excused himself, stepping several feet away. Not recognizing the number, he answered. "Kelman."

"Jake?" The caller coughed into the phone.

"Is this you, Mr. Magnus?"

"Yes. I want you to come over to my ranch as soon as possible. We need to talk."

He checked the time. Three o'clock. "I can come as soon as I'm finished here. Probably around six. Will that be all right?"

"No. I need to see you right away. Within the hour would be best."

"Let me speak with Wyatt. I'm sure I can work out something."

"Good. I'll expect you soon."

"Yes, sir." Ending the call, Jake scanned the room for Wyatt, spotting him across the room. Hurrying toward him, hoping no one noticed the urgency, he stopped next to Wyatt and his wife, Daisy.

"Hey, Jake. I wanted to tell you how beautiful the tree is this year. Almost too perfect." Daisy chuckled.

"Thanks. Jimmy found it, and we all voted on it. The selection was a group effort. Wyatt, do you have a minute?"

"Sure. I'll be back in a minute, sweetheart." Kissing Daisy's cheek, he joined Jake several feet away. "What do you need?"

"A couple hours off. Seth Magnus called. He needs to see me right away. The truth is, he didn't sound so good on the phone."

"What did he want?"

"He wouldn't tell me. Insisted on seeing me at the ranch as soon as possible."

Wyatt's brows furrowed in concern. "Maybe I should go with you."

"You're welcome to come."

Rubbing the back of his neck, Wyatt gave a slow shake of his head. "Nah. I'll stay here so you two can talk freely. Call if I need to drive over."

"Will do. I'll be back as soon as I can."

"Take as long as you need, Jake. We've got things covered here."

"Thanks, Wyatt."

Shoving his arms into his warmest coat, he headed outside to his truck. Saying a prayer the weather would hold for a few hours, he drove to the Magnus Ranch. Several cars and trucks were parked in an open area to the right of the house. Strange, as the ranch hands parked next to the bunkhouse. Shoving the thought away, he parked, bounding up the front steps. The door opened as he reached it.

"Are you Jake?" A thirtyish red-haired woman with a ready smile looked him up and down.

"Yes, ma'am."

"I'm his daughter-in-law. Come in. He's been fretting the last hour about seeing you."

He was about to ask her name when she continued.

"Follow me. Sorry about the house being full of people. Seth asked us to come over and take a few things each of us wants. Kind of an odd way to give away your belongings, but Seth has never been conventional."

Following her down a hall, they took the stairs to the second floor. Turning right, she motioned him to the bedroom at the front of the house.

"He's in there. I'll be downstairs when you're ready to leave." She whirled around, heading downstairs before he could thank her.

Knocking, a gravelly voice responded. "Is that you, Jake? If it's anyone else, go away."

Stifling a chuckle, he entered the bedroom. "It's me, Mr. Magnus."

"Good. Sit down. And call me Seth."

"Yes, sir. Uh...Seth." Picking up a stack of books from a chair, he set them on a desk before sitting down. "I came as soon as I could." He found Magnus sitting up in his large bed, a book on his lap.

"We have a problem."

Jake's stomach plummeted. "What is it?"

"I'm still selling you the ranch. I don't go back on my word."

"That's real good to hear."

"The fact is, I've already signed the papers. You'll be getting a call from the banker about signing your set this week. My suggestion is you sign as soon as possible."

"All right. Can you tell me why the rush?"

"Something unexpected is responsible for pushing this through." Leaning forward, he coughed several times before straightening.

Standing, Jake took a step toward the bed. "Can I get you water or anything?"

Seth held up his hand. "I'm fine."

Nodding, he sat back down. "Tell me what's so urgent."

"The bottom line is, I'm dying."

Chapter Twenty-Four

Jake couldn't stop his jaw from dropping. "Dying? You seem so healthy. Well, until now anyway."

"I've been fighting this cancer for ten years. Seems there's nothing more they can do. The doctor gives me a few weeks, maybe two months. You see how important it is to get all my business dealings wrapped up." Coughing again, he grabbed a tissue. "I thought there was more time. A year or two at least. Your offer to purchase the ranch, well...it will ease my mind to know the land and operations will go to someone who appreciates it."

Clearing his throat, Jake couldn't think of anything to say. What does one say to a man who's dying?

"I assume you still want to go ahead with buying the place?"

"Yes, sir. More than anything. It's just tough knowing you won't be around to see how my plans play out."

Face brightening, Seth sat straighter. "Tell me about those plans."

"If you're sure."

"Wouldn't ask if I wasn't. Now, lay it all out there."

For the next hour, Jake explained his idea of adding Black Wagyu cattle to the ranch. Seth listened, excitement flashing in his still alert eyes.

"Have you thought of raising bison?"

He grinned. "It crossed my mind. The climate and terrain are fine, and I understand the demand is rising."

"It's interesting how eating any kind of beef was tabu for a while. My understanding is it's experiencing a revival. Your plans fit right into the change in demand."

They spoke another hour, brainstorming the pros and cons of various ventures. When Jake thought he'd taken enough of Seth's time, the older man made one last comment.

"You know, we used to have a ranch rodeo here every summer. Anson took it over for a couple years, and I know he does a small rodeo for his dude ranch. The ranch rodeo brought in a lot of people from out of the area. Turned out to be a good way to introduce them to our prime beef. You might consider if it would help with your plans to expand operations."

Jake didn't have to think about it long. Ranch rodeos could be the piece of the puzzle he'd been missing. The piece making everything else fall into place.

The short drive back to Whistle Rock Ranch didn't last long enough for him to list everything he had to do. Seth's prognosis changed Jake's plans regarding the next six months.

Talking to Wyatt and Virgil would be his first priority. He still had to decide what to tell Beth. She'd become important to him, a woman he wanted to stay in his life.

Spotting the two men who governed his future at Whistle Rock, he covered the ground between them with minimal steps. Each man's features were severe. He guessed they discussed Jimmy.

"Hey, Jake." Virgil shifted toward him. "How'd it go with Seth?"

Shoving his hands in the pockets of his jeans, he shook his head. "I don't know if you've heard, but Seth has been fighting cancer for years. The doctors have told him there's nothing more they can do. They've given him a few weeks. Maybe a couple months. That's why he wanted to talk with me."

"I hadn't heard anything about him being ill. I wonder if Pop knows." Wyatt raised his head to look toward the lodge.

"The way Seth spoke, I doubt anyone knows outside his family."

"Stubborn as always," Wyatt said. "What's the status of the sale?"

"He wants to go forward, with it closing by the end of December."

Wyatt gave a knowing nod. "Makes sense. Can you do that, Jake?"

"I've already called the person who manages my money. According to her, it won't be a problem. My issue now is hiring a foreman. Seth was going to run the ranch for several months while I identified the right person to take over. Obviously, that's no longer an option."

Virgil pulled out his phone, scrolling through the contacts. "I may know of someone. He sent me an email not long ago. Said he was ready to move back to Wyoming."

Jake worked to curb his excitement. "Where is he now?"

"Idaho. He's been the foreman at a ranch raising angus cattle." Virgil glanced up. "Might be a perfect fit for you. I'll get in touch to see if he can make a trip down here."

"Soon." Jake grinned.

"Right." Calling, Virgil waited. "Quinn. It's Virgil. I have a job opportunity which may be perfect for you. It's at an angus ranch next door to Whistle Rock. Are you available to come down for a few days? Great. We have a cabin where you can stay. See you then."

Ending the call, Virgil slid the phone away. "We caught him at a good time. He'll be here tomorrow."

"How long can he stay?" Jake asked.

"Two, maybe three days. With his experience, that should be enough time for the two of you to decide if he's a fit."

"Tell me about him."

"His name's Quinn Sawyer. We met at the University of Wyoming. He was born on a ranch outside of Sheridan. After graduation, he headed back up there. I don't know how he ended up in Idaho."

"I'll ask him," Jake said.

"I believe he has a business degree in ranch and livestock management. Not married. No real ties to Idaho that I know about." Virgil looked at Wyatt. "I told him we could put him up in a cabin."

"No problem. I'll let Mom know. I'm going to find Pop. He'll want to know about Seth. It's so hard to believe. Always thought he'd be around forever." Wyatt took off for the lodge, his usual straight posture slumped in the shoulders.

Jake watched him walk away. "Any news on Jimmy?"

"He'll be able to return to the ranch this afternoon. I'm waiting for the call."

"Do you want me to go with you?"

"Thanks, Jake. What you can do is check on how the training is going. Barrel and Brady have been working in the far corral."

"Sure, Virgil. Do you have another minute? There's one more issue I'd like to discuss."

Jake's lack of sleep caught up with him as he dressed the next morning. Exhaustion had become normal in his life. The conversation with Seth had impacted him more than he'd expected.

He'd thought the grizzled rancher would be around for years, imparting his knowledge and providing ideas.

Knowing the man for such a short period of time, his absence would be a significant loss.

He had a brief call with Quinn the prior evening. His potential foreman was expected to arrive at the ranch by eleven in the morning. They'd questioned each other over basics. At the end, he'd felt good about Virgil's recommendation. In a few hours, he'd meet the man in person.

Jake's short talk with Virgil about an idea developed with Seth had gone well. They'd even discussed a few details and possible timing before Jake headed to the horse corral.

The morning passed with none of the interruptions experienced the last few days. Jimmy tried to do his work, only to find the other ranch hands taking care of the chores for him.

At fifteen minutes before ten, Quinn Sawyer pulled into the ranch. The two-ton Chevy truck indicated how serious he took his work.

Jake greeted him, extending a hand. "You must be Quinn. I'm Jake Kelman."

"Good to meet you. So this is Whistle Rock Ranch. Always wanted to see it in person. Virgil built it up a lot when we were in college. Doesn't appear he exaggerated."

"The Bonner family has built it into an enviable operation with the help of Virgil and his father, Jasper." Jake explained how Jasper and his wife, Monica, were on an extended vacation. "They're expected back soon. How about I show you around this ranch, then we'll head over to the Magnus spread?"

"Sounds good."

"First, I'll show you your cabin and get you some food."

"No need to get me food, Jake. I brought sandwiches with me. I'd prefer to spend my time on the Magnus Ranch."

Quinn dropped his bag in the cabin, washed his face and hands, then joined Jake outside. "These cabins are for the guests during the summer?"

"They are. We're building a few more this spring to accommodate the growth in interest. The guests who were here last summer talked it up to their friends. We're almost full for next year's season, and that includes the increase in cabins."

"Impressive. Do they still operate the horse breeding and cattle businesses?"

"Sure do. The registered quarter horse and Paint horse operation has grown each year. They receive orders from all over for their equines. Wyatt and Virgil are in charge of the horse breeding and sales business. I'm handling the cattle operation, and managing the guest ranch business."

"Which is why you're looking for a foreman at the Magnus place."

"Correct. I'll be involved, but you'd be running day-to-day operations. Does that fit with what you see for yourself?"

A broad smile brightened Quinn's features. "Fits great."

"Let's get over to Seth's ranch. I'm hoping he's doing well enough to meet you. We'll take my truck."

Beth stood at the kitchen window, watching Jake show a man around Whistle Rock. After rounding the barn, they climbed into Jake's truck, driving off toward the ranch down the road.

They'd spoken for a few minutes each day after meals. Beth knew he was involved in a project at a nearby ranch, though she had no idea what.

She didn't recognize the man with Jake. The truck had an Idaho license plate, which meant little nowadays. People moved around more frequently than in previous generations. He did look as if he made his living on a ranch.

Beth turned toward where Abigail worked on assembling enchiladas for lunch. Paired with rice, beans, and chips, the ranch hands would have just enough room for brownies, cookies, and cobbler.

"Have you heard anything about the activities at the ranch next door?"

Straightening, Abigail's expression gave nothing away. "They raise angus beef and sell it to restaurants. Oh, and it's owned by a longtime Wyoming family. Why?"

"No reason, except I've seen Jake drive in that direction several times over the last week."

"Probably nothing, Beth. Virgil and Wyatt have him doing all kinds of things. If it worries you, maybe you should ask him."

"Absolutely not. If he wants me to know, he'll tell me." She joined Abigail at the work counter. "All right. What still needs to be done before the boys arrive for lunch?"

Chapter Twenty-Five

"What do you think, Quinn? Would you be willing to quit your job in Idaho to run this place?" Jake had known within thirty minutes the man beside him in the truck was the perfect person to run his ranch. They'd already talked numbers, and he knew Quinn had no problem with the pay.

"How soon do you want me to start?"

"Is that a yes, you'll take the job?"

"If it was an offer, then my answer is yes. I've already given notice. All I'd have to do is drive back to pack my things. There isn't much, mainly clothes, books, pictures, tack, and my horse. I can be back here before Christmas."

"Great. As Seth said, the foreman's place is behind the main house. We should've looked it over before leaving."

"No problem, Jake. I'm sure it will be fine."

"I'll make sure it's clean before you get back. Is the twentieth a good date for you to arrive?"

"Might be the eighteenth, if that's all right."

"Hey. Any day you choose before Christmas is good for me. I'd appreciate it if you kept me posted on your schedule." Parking, Jake got out, nodding toward the lodge. "It's time to eat. Let's get some food before it's gone."

The tables in the dining room had changed since breakfast, replaced by long, rectangular tables for fourteen. Jake found a spot at the table closest to the kitchen.

After introducing Quinn, they filled their plates with chicken enchiladas, beef tacos, and chiles rellenos. Their food was piled high enough to force the use of additional plates for their beans and rice.

"Chips, guacamole, and sour cream are always in bowls on the table." The words had barely left Jake's mouth when Beth emerged from the kitchen. She held a tray filled with small bowls of guacamole and sour cream. Her smile widened when she spotted Jake.

"Is that the cook?" Quinn set down his plate and sat down.

"Beth, and she's the head chef."

"Chef, huh?" Picking up a taco, he ate half of it with one bite. "This is great. I don't know what she did, but it's amazing."

"She attended culinary school before getting jobs at some major restaurants in Wyoming."

"Why leave a restaurant job to cook for a bunch of ranch hands?"

"Beth's from here. Her mother has some medical issues, so Beth decided it was best to return to Brilliance. This job fit her needs, and we get to benefit from her culinary skills."

Taking a bite of the chiles rellenos, Quinn growled in pleasure. "This is incredible. Does my job include coming over here once in a while for dinner?"

Chuckling, Jake scooped up some beans and rice. "I'm sure we can work something out."

"Hello, gentlemen. Hope you're enjoying your meal."

"This is great, ma'am. I'm glad Jake invited me."

"I'm Beth."

When he moved to stand, she held up her hand, motioning him to stay seated. "Nice to meet you. I'm Quinn."

"Are you a new ranch hand?"

"Sure am, or will be soon." He glanced at Jake.

"Well, nice to meet you." Her smile softened when she looked at Jake. "See you a little later?"

"Count on it."

When she was out of earshot, Quinn leaned toward Jake. "So that's how it is."

"Yep. I'm a lucky man. Thanks for being discreet about the job."

"You said just a few people knew what was going on. I figured it was best not to say more than necessary. So Beth does this all by herself?"

"She has an assistant. My sister. She started working here several weeks ago."

"Your sister must be real good to work with Beth. Does she have formal training, too?"

"Not that I know about. This job has been just what she needed. How about some dessert?"

"I never pass up the chance for homemade dessert. Is that cobbler?"

"Sure looks like it." Jake filled a bowl with the cherry confection, handing it to Quinn. "Ice cream and spoons are right over there."

It didn't take either long to finish their cobblers. Quinn waved off coffee, deciding he'd head to the cabin for some sleep. Thanking Jake again, he slipped on his jacket, stepping into a light snow.

Passing the kitchen window, he glanced inside. Two women stood talking. Except the short, dark haired one appeared familiar. Staring a moment longer, he shook his head. It wasn't her, he was certain of it.

That woman was miles away, cooking in a little diner a block off the highway. And Quinn Sawyer was the last person she'd ever want to see.

Reaching out, Jake took Beth's hand in his. It had turned into another beautiful, clear night. The light snow had stopped, the temperature warming enough so their noses didn't sting. Changing directions, he led her into the barn.

"What are we doing in here?"

"We need to talk, Beth."

"That doesn't sound good."

"I hope it isn't bad. Let's go sit on the workbench."

"It's not big enough for both of us, Jake."

"That's all right. I'm going to stand."

Her stomach turned sour. She remembered Freddie, the night he told her they could no longer be friends. After he explained, she agreed.

"All right."

"Remember when I told you about wanting to buy a ranch?"

"Of course."

"What I didn't tell you was I already had the money saved. It was money I earned rodeoing."

"People make that kind of money competing?"

"There are a good many who made a lot more than me. Trace was one of them."

"All right." She couldn't help wondering where this conversation was going. "So you have the money to buy a ranch. Do you know where?"

"Sure do. An opportunity came up right here in Brilliance. In fact, it's the Magnus Ranch, right next door to Whistle Rock."

Her eyes grew wide. "You bought it?"

"The deal will finalize by the end of this month. Seth raises angus cattle. The beef is sold to high-end restaurants in Wyoming, Montana, and Idaho. There are many other opportunities."

Clasping her hands in her lap, she tried to wrap her mind around Jake buying a ranch to the west of Whistle Rock.

"That's wonderful news, Jake. I'm so happy for you. Does this have anything to do with Quinn?"

"He's the key to making it all work. Quinn is a friend of Virgil's. He'll be my foreman so I can honor my commitment to the Bonners. I've spoken with Anson, Wyatt, Margie, and Virgil. They're all a hundred percent behind the plan. My commitment to them is two years. I'll live at my ranch and work here."

"So we'll be able to see each other once in a while."

"Beth, I'm hoping we'll see each other a lot more than once in a while."

"I don't understand."

Kneeling beside the bench, he reached out, taking her hands in his. "We haven't known each other long, but I love you, Beth. I can't imagine a life without you in it. Marry me. We'll fulfill all our dreams...together." Reaching into his pocket, he pulled out a small velvet pouch, retrieving a ring with a beautiful diamond. "Will you marry me, Beth?"

Glancing into his eyes, seeing sincerity and love, she nodded. With tears streaming down her cheeks, she wrapped her arms around him.

"I love you, Jake. Yes, I'll marry you."

Slipping the ring on her finger, he took her into his arms, pressing a warm kiss onto her mouth. Leaning back, he was surprised to see a question in her eyes.

"What about your dream of riding in a rodeo one more time? I don't want you to give up on it because of me."

Swiping tears from her cheeks, he cupped her face in both hands. "I have a plan for achieving that dream as well."

"Are you going to tell me what it is?"

"You'll just have to trust me for a little while. Can you do that?"

Kissing his lips, she smiled. "I'm trusting you with the rest of my life, and that includes whatever comes next."

Epilogue

"Come on, Jake! You've got this!" Beth shouted from her seat at the National Western Stock Show Rodeo held in Denver every January. "Stay on!"

Sitting on both sides of her were Wyatt, Daisy, Virgil, and Lily. All were yelling encouragement as if Jake could hear them. As the timer ticked closer to eight seconds, their voices grew louder.

When the buzzer sounded, Jake jumped from the saddlebronc to the ground, rolled, and came up with both hands in the air. He'd done it. Completed his rides in the saddlebronc and bareback categories.

"He's in the top three of each." Wyatt clapped and yelled above the roar of the crowd. "What a comeback!"

"Let's hear it for Jake Kelman." The announcer revved up support from the crowd. "An incredible achievement after two years out of the circuit." Again, the crowd roared.

Swiping tears of joy and relief from her face, Beth stood, waving the Wyoming flag in the air. Seeing it, Jake took off his hat, brandishing it in their direction.

The Denver rodeo had been the final item on the bucket list he'd created months earlier. Looking back over the last few weeks, Beth had to smile at the progression of events since he'd asked her to marry him.

Margie's Christmas party had been an incredible success. Beth's dishes received compliments from the guests, some people requesting the recipes, which she politely declined.

Less than two weeks later, Jake and Beth announced their engagement on Christmas Eve. Theirs would be a casual wedding with friends, family, and those at the ranch in attendance on New Year's Eve. When Margie offered to help with the arrangements, Beth had gratefully accepted.

A week to plan and execute a wedding was a grand achievement. The ceremony and reception had gone off without a single problem.

The New Year had marched in with just one little hitch.

The sound of yet another vehicle pulling into the ranch for the wedding drew Abigail's attention to the window. A man emerged from a truck she didn't recognize. Hat low, collar pulled up against the wind, he looked up for a moment, then at the ground as he made his way to the lodge's front door.

Abigail edged forward, body tensing.

"Who is he, Abbie?" Daisy strained to get a good look at the man.

She and Lily had volunteered to help in the kitchen so Beth could enjoy her wedding day. The two women, energetic and flexible, had been exactly what Abigail needed.

"Um…I don't know for sure." But in her heart, she did know.

Lily squeezed in between them. "You know, I think he's the man Jake hired as foreman at his ranch. He's a friend of Virgil's. I think he came down from Idaho."

Idaho. The name had Abigail's stomach clenching.

Daisy felt her friend tense beside her. Studying Abigail, she saw how her face had drained of color. "Are you all right?"

No, I'm not. "Fine. This is the first time I've been in charge of an event this size."

"You're doing great," Lily said, placing a hand on Abigail's arm. "Are you certain you're all right?"

"Everything's good. Thanks." Picking up a tray laden with appetizers, she hesitated a moment before pushing the door to the dining room open.

She told herself there was no way he could recognize her. Not with her hair cut shorter, and the bottle blonde replaced with her natural, warm brown locks. She'd also lost weight in the two years they'd been apart. No, there wasn't a chance the man who'd left her behind would recognize her on a ranch in southern Wyoming.

Sipping a beer, Quinn watched as a woman emerged from the kitchen. Carrying a large tray of appetizers, she smiled as she set it on the buffet table before returning to the kitchen.

Quinn's jaw dropped, his mind spinning. It was the woman he'd seen through the kitchen window the day he'd met Jake. The woman with short, brown hair. A woman more slender than the one from his past who came to mind.

In his heart, he knew it was the same woman he'd fallen in love with, then left behind for a job.

Learn about upcoming books in **The Cowboys of Whistle Rock Ranch** series at shirleendavies.com.

Enjoy the Whistle Rock cowboys? You might want to read Macklins of Whiskey Bend.

If you want to keep current on all my preorders, new releases, and other happenings, sign up for my newsletter at http://www.shirleendavies.com/contact-me.html

A Note from Shirleen

Thank you for taking the time to reading The Cowboy's Final Ride!

Leave a Review! If you enjoyed the, please consider posting a short review and telling your friends. Word of mouth is an author's best friend and much appreciated.

I care about quality, so if you find something in error, please contact me via email at shirleen@shirleendavies.com

Books by Shirleen Davies

<u>Contemporary Western Romance Series</u>

MacLarens of Fire Mountain

Second Summer, Book One
Hard Landing, Book Two
One More Day, Book Three
All Your Nights, Book Four
Always Love You, Book Five
Hearts Don't Lie, Book Six
No Getting Over You, Book Seven
'Til the Sun Comes Up, Book Eight
Foolish Heart, Book Nine

Macklins of Whiskey Bend

Thorn, Book One
Del, Book Two
Boone, Book Three
Kell, Book Four
Zane, Book Five
Josh, Book Six, Coming Next in the Series!

Cowboys of Whistle Rock Ranch

The Cowboy's Road Home, Book One
The Cowboy's False Start, Book Two
The Cowboy's Second Chance Family, Book Three
The Cowboy's Final Ride, Book Four
The Cowboy's Surprise Reunion, Book Five, Coming
Next in the Series!

Historical Western Romance Series
Redemption Mountain

Redemption's Edge, Book One
Wildfire Creek, Book Two
Sunrise Ridge, Book Three
Dixie Moon, Book Four
Survivor Pass, Book Five
Promise Trail, Book Six
Deep River, Book Seven
Courage Canyon, Book Eight
Forsaken Falls, Book Nine
Solitude Gorge, Book Ten
Rogue Rapids, Book Eleven
Angel Peak, Book Twelve
Restless Wind, Book Thirteen
Storm Summit, Book Fourteen
Mystery Mesa, Book Fifteen
Thunder Valley, Book Sixteen

A Very Splendor Christmas, Holiday Novella, Book
Seventeen
Paradise Point, Book Eighteen,
Silent Sunset, Book Nineteen
Rocky Basin, Book Twenty
Captive Dawn, Book Twenty-One, Coming Next in the
Series!

MacLarens of Fire Mountain

Tougher than the Rest, Book One
Faster than the Rest, Book Two
Harder than the Rest, Book Three
Stronger than the Rest, Book Four
Deadlier than the Rest, Book Five
Wilder than the Rest, Book Six

MacLarens of Boundary Mountain

Colin's Quest, Book One,
Brodie's Gamble, Book Two
Quinn's Honor, Book Three
Sam's Legacy, Book Four
Heather's Choice, Book Five
Nate's Destiny, Book Six
Blaine's Wager, Book Seven
Fletcher's Pride, Book Eight
Bay's Desire, Book Nine
Cam's Hope, Book Ten

Romantic Suspense

Eternal Brethren, Military Romantic Suspense

Steadfast, Book One
Shattered, Book Two
Haunted, Book Three
Untamed, Book Four
Devoted, Book Five
Faithful, Book Six
Exposed, Book Seven
Undaunted, Book Eight
Resolute, Book Nine
Unspoken, Book Ten
Defiant, Book Eleven

Peregrine Bay, Romantic Suspense

Reclaiming Love, Book One
Our Kind of Love, Book Two

Find all of my books at:
https://www.shirleendavies.com/books.html

About Shirleen

Shirleen Davies writes romance—historical and contemporary western romance, and romantic suspense. She grew up in Southern California, attended Oregon State University, and has degrees from San Diego State University and the University of Maryland. During the day she provides consulting services to small and mid-sized businesses. But her real passion is writing emotionally charged stories of flawed people who find redemption through love and acceptance. She now lives with her husband in a beautiful town in northern Arizona.

I love to hear from my readers!

Send me an email: shirleen@shirleendavies.com
Visit my Website: https://www.shirleendavies.com/
Sign up to be notified of New Releases:
https://www.shirleendavies.com/contact/
Follow me on Amazon:
http://www.amazon.com/author/shirleendavies
Follow me on BookBub:
https://www.bookbub.com/authors/shirleen-davies

Other ways to connect with me:

Facebook Author Page:
http://www.facebook.com/shirleendaviesauthor
Pinterest: http://pinterest.com/shirleendavies

Instagram:
https://www.instagram.com/shirleendavies_author/
TikTok: shirleendavies_author
Twitter: www.twitter.com/shirleendavies